Paper Edition
Continuous Printing
First Published December 1, 2023
Issue "E" 02/18/2026

Library of Congress
Control Number: 2018907716

ISBN: 9780983857587

Published by

WEST WINTER PRESS
Sky Valley, California, USA

Acknowledgements
Page 91 "Embrace, that was convulsion ..."
From the novel *Aurora Leigh* by
Elizabeth Barrett Browning, 1856

Page 178 "There is a solitude..."
From the essay "The Solitude of the Self" by
Elizabeth Cady Stanton, 1892

jane nineteen

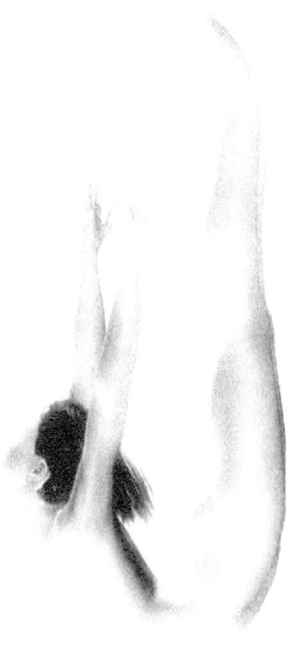

an erotic novel by
j.j.kirnan

From the Author

This tale came to me as a discovery. I found it.

My inclination to vivify the American West at the end of the nineteenth century, and to portray a first love, turned tumultuous.

This became Jane.

I dare not write her from afar. Nothing seeming. She knows how to fire a rifle, after all.

John Kirnan
Sonoran Desert, California
Summer 2023

Sexual Content Advisory and Promise:

This book contains expansive and explicit depiction of lovemaking with passion and consent.

part 1
april 1897

lovely sated breath
and body

j.j.kirnan

April 10, 1897
Saturday
Seven miles West of Silver City, New Mexico

Out a two-day ride from the herding range, Jane
fought the dust.

She had water. A creaking windmill pulled it up from
the aquifer below. No stream or lake for four miles, so the
flow from deep must never fail. She could irrigate the
garden, wash clothes and dishes – and attend her slight
body and cascading black hair, to keep fresh, a treasure to
abide cleanliness by abundant cool water.

Otherwise, the dust would win. She never complained
of the battle. He endured hardships in the valley of the
Gila River? She would fight the elements on this little
place east of two hills. Today, the wind retreated, and so
likewise her war with every mote that seeped through
planks of the house when it blew.

Jane walked out into the spring morning, determined
to enlarge the planting ground.

What? Between the first two strokes of the spade,
something. She held her breath quiet. Yes. Yes. A horse.
In five seconds, the certainty – his horse – a familiar hitch
in its gait and a faint jingle. She dropped the shovel and
ran to the edge of the inner fence, gazing with hand above
eyes, westward, out along the path winding between the
two hills. The clatter of hooves on dry earth increased, an
animal at half-stride.

She saw him.

A quarter mile down the trail, soon two hundred
yards, his horse now urged to full gallop, noise and
rumble rolling ahead, his unsmiling gaze locked onto hers.

Then, the vault off the animal as it skidded to a halt.

He freed the horse from saddle and packs in five seconds
and leapt over the outer fence. Dust swarmed off his shirt
and leather vest. Jane sidestepped toward the porch and
front door, stumbling in surety of his will blasting across
the yard. He bolted through the inner fence gate,
throwing off hat, squirming out of vest, chapped pants
swishing harshly.

He nearly caught her outside. She escaped through
the door and raced two rooms in, taking a stand at the
bed. When he reached the bedroom, her work dress went
flying off towards him onto the floor. Otherwise – it
would have been ripped to shreds.

They crashed together. He might wrench the life out
of her, stop her breath with his massive embrace, lifting
her body straight off the floor.

She pulled his head against her breasts. They heated
through the undershirt with the roar of his voice. He
threw her on the bed and stood above in confidence while
yanking off shirt, pulling boots to kick them away, spurs
spinning wild. He gripped the waist of his trousers – and
stopped.

The only motion in the room ... her hand easing
down, slipping under the waistband of the cotton
undergarment, caressing there – there between thighs, the
slush of wet flesh under touch of fingers gorgeous in the
silence.

In her eyes, sweetness gone carnal.

And a flash of arrogance.

"Might we help you, sir?" All blooming and sauce.

He grabbed her wrist and yanked the hand away.
Seizing the hem of the garment, he tore it from her hips
with a violent ripping sound. She screeched like a captive.
Her body arched high and thudded down. Instantly he

pushed her legs up to her chest.

"Open," he ordered.

She fit hands behind thighs, pulled back and apart, folding her body until knees touched the quilt. The gleaming vee rose from the bed, lips separating tenderly. Jane's eyes fluttered to bear the exquisite exposure, naked with danger, raging, delicious.

He pulled range-pants down, took organ in hand, stroked it to full erection. Her gaze clung to it in the inexorable reality unfolding.

Tip poised between lips.

Body coiled.

Muscles in arms and back bulged.

Cock thrust into liquid girl.

"Oh no no no no no," she bellowed.

Penetrated, pinned, she squirmed and squealed – but urged him deeper – pulling thighs aside, rotating hips to get cock rock-solid home.

"Nail me to this bed," she whispered.

His hips pulled back – he drove forward with all his weight – she screamed to the sky.

"Yes. Yes. Yes. Put all the lonely fucking in me."

He must have been insane, five weeks in the wild, away. Hungry, ravenous – mad with wrath like wildfire on the prairie. He could not speak, only stroke, with a ragged grunt on each. Every blow thudded her hips into the bed.

"... thousand times," she said. "There. There. There."

He moved up the bed for a better angle. The next thrust reamed fully, drove deep, dragging the bud along.

"No. No. No. Oh my God in heaven. No. No. No."

"Shut up."

"Fuck me. There. There. Fuck me. Fuck me. There.

There. There."

Then, his eyes found hers. She drank the magnificent ferocity in them – the sweet, crushing, lust-drive of her man.

Taking her.

~~~~~

"Rode like the wind."

He nodded. "The animal thought I was mad."

They sat on the bed face to face. She had made a quick run to wash, returning with a towel for him. She glanced down at his boots on the floor, her shredded bottoms draped across the spurs. He had not ripped her camisole off. She liked having it on, like a joke.

"How long?"

"Left before dawn yesterday."

"It's a two-day ride."

"Not this time."

She went silent, with an eloquent smile. He caught it.

"Woman, you are all vanity to make a man crazy for you."

She kept the smile and nodded her head twice.

"I was only greedy for the good butter put up in the cellar, and new bread."

"Right," Jane said.

"The big bathtub."

"Right."

"A bed instead of something thrown on the ground."

"Right. Nothing else." Her eyes filled. Morning light glinted in them.

The banter stopped. She trembled, knowing his mind, knowing he would say the next awful thing. His eyes dominated, keeping her silent, transfixed by his intention.

"Driven mad to get your cunt."

Sweet humiliation. Her nostrils flared. Her breath caught on that word. That word. His saying it opened her good as if pushing thighs apart.

"Yes," she whispered, cheeks flushing.

"Say it."

"No."

"You are proud of it, now say it."

"No."

An adorable stubbornness defended her modesty. Both knew it was contrived.

He tugged at the hem of her shirt. She pushed his hand away. She took the fringe of the garment between fingers. The phallus jerked alive. He took rod in hand.

"Slow," he said.

Her eyes flashed. She lifted the shirt. As the nubs came into view, he stroked himself erect. She pulled the garment off.

"Touch," he ordered.

Hands moved with grace, fitting under rounded flesh. She raised them, offered them, tantalized with them – as if precious fruits from a sacred garden – that he might feast his eyes for seconds, seconds, on sweet breasts. She moved them slowly, subtly changing their shape, telling their softness. She waited until his gaze came up, then spoke the aching truth ...

"Yes. I did. I did make you ride like the wind. To get my cunt."

He slid his body to her side. One hand eased hers away and covered a breast. His mouth fit onto hers. Jane's free hand went to the back of his neck and pulled, urging his kissing to fill her mouth. She slipped tongue over his, to let him slide in the wet. His hand on her breast claimed possession yet sent affection and desire without cruelty – and such ungentle tenderness is cruel.

Jane melted into the bed. He used his advantage to rotate her head, placing kisses where he wanted them. She let go all resistence – her hand in his hair only to feel his every movement. He caressed her breasts and roamed her mouth with his for minutes.

He pulled back.

"You did not get yours yet," he said.

"Keep kissing me."

"Your explosion."

"It's okay."

"No, it is not."

"Take your pleasure again," Jane said with laughing eyes.

"No."

"Put it in me. Take your pleasure again. That's all I want."

She could barely hold his gaze. With no sex for weeks, Jane reverted to "shy" in places. Brazen in some, shy in others. With their many partings and greetings, they had learned to expect this retreat, and now played it with delight – his touch must seek her folded-away cravings as if brand-new seduction.

His gaze fixed her. It did not vary as he removed his hand from her breast and trailed it down her belly, reaching for the conjunction, settling in place. Jane exhaled sharply.

"No," she said.

"Your favorite word."

"No, don't."

"Open."

"Oh no oh no."

"My hand belongs here."

The shy thighs parted. His fingers moved slowly.

"The softest thing in the world," he said.

"Don't," she said, laughing with nervousness and delight at the same time.

"I thought of this every night for five weeks. Putting my hand here."

"Don't touch inside."

"It drove me mad, wanting it in my hand."

"Oh ..."

"To stir the wet."

"Don't go inside."

"If you forbid it, I will make you put *your* fingers in."

"Never!"

"I know you touched it every night."

"I never touched it."

"Yes, you did. You put your fingers in. All the way in. You rubbed and pushed deep until you exploded. Every night."

"Yes."

"Yes what?"

"Yes, I touched myself."

"Until it erupted like a fountain."

"It's your fault. Two years ago, I was a chaste nineteen-year-old girl who could well do without, but your big prick has made it hungry all the time." She was twenty-one now, he twenty-six.

He eased the lips apart, slipped two fingers to the opening, and penetrated.

"Oh fuck fuck fuck," she cried.

"And then I taught you to say that word."

"Fuck!"

Soon Jane could not speak. His fingers controlled. His intention did not tease – its plan was plain as a plum. The hand was relentless. The other cradled her head, insistent that it not turn away. He stroked and caressed between her legs, finding every part wanting, spreading the wetness along her thighs, under to the round bottom cheeks, even up through the thin black hair to the bottom of her belly. Yet always returning to the softest thing in the world.

"Ya, ya, ma, ya, oh, oh ..." her incoherent voice gurgled up from some cavern in her chest newly disturbed. "Oh, fee, oh, oh, oh ..."

His touch grew stronger. She bore the increase with louder moans. The shudders began, emanating from the deep pelvis.

"Now!" He slid down the bed. Her legs flew wide. He grasped behind each knee and pushed. Her bottom rose off the bed, the trembling sex opened, gleaming with juice, swollen and begging.

His mouth plunged forward.

"Oh fuck fuck fuck fuck fuck," she screamed.

Pinned in place, she could not defend the horrible invasion. His lips would not let go the bud. His tongue would not stop thrusting into vagina. Lips and tongue pressed together, capturing the organ of pleasure inside and out, claiming it like a conqueror. He drank her, licked her, ate her raw.

"Oh my God in heaven oh oh oh oh oh."

When the true shudder began, when a ball of tension appeared, the abandon in his act went racing away. His mouth roamed her crazily, sucking on every crease and fold – to lure the erotic orb out of her pelvis – to kiss it open and vault her to the infinite. Her body arched up, legs split apart wider than ever, and she wiggled full force against his mouth.

"Oh fuck oh fucking oh ..."

All the femme organs seized and shook. The flood of juice filled his mouth. He let it drain onto the bed. Convulsions racked her body, which never ceased its thrust onto him.

She could not speak. Her body trembled. One leg, released from his grip, rattled on the bed. Her hand fit behind his head and pulled hard, urging his glorious mouth to suck forever.

Like the patient man of the West he was, he pulled off and waited.

"Ride down slow," he said.

It was beautiful to watch. Her skin glowed. The scent of female after-sex filled the room like earth perfume. She sighed. She giggled. Sometimes she looked in his eyes – with a smile all happy women have known. Then her arms and legs flopped on the bed, helpless with lovely sated breath and body.

He stirred and edged up next to her on one elbow. In her creamy dream, she did not notice. Then, the press of his organ on her thigh ...

"Oh."

"Yes."

"Go ahead. Take your pleasure," she said, exasperated.

"I hope you will always say that."

"I will. It's a woman's damn duty."

The cock twitched.

"Open your legs again."

"I can't. That took everything out of me. I'm melted."

"Your duty as woman."

She did not laugh, knowing the next thing would be

drama. She willed it so in her heart. Slowly, with grim erotic intent, she spread herself open on the bed. Achingly slow. An act of unmitigated sex-love, woman opening to man. She held his eyes, beckoning.

He moved carefully into place. Her arms folded around his neck. He lowered himself. She caught the scent of her sex on his mouth. As the first thrust slipped into her body, she kissed his lips and wrapped her legs around her man.

~~~~~

The sun filtering through shaded windows called them out of bed.

He swiveled out first, made a run outside. Jane lay still, peaceful, satisfied. She did not care if the corners of the cabin were dusty, or not. When he returned, she watched as he dressed. Medium-height frame, five inches taller than her. Taut muscles well defined. Erect posture. Chest broader than expected. Hirsute – a shock of unruly hair the color of a chestnut infused with a slight auburn taint. From mid-belly across to his left side and up almost a foot, an evil-looking scar blazed white against the browned skin of his torso. His face – impossible to steady on one heritage alone – indescribable in the glow of her satisfaction. Rather ... beyond description. She believed it *stern odd rough handsome sweet wild dangerous.*

He pulled over a shirt of homespun which tied with leather stringers, and a loose pair of wool trousers, blue. The socks were store-bought, but not the belt around his middle – she had made it.

He regarded her on the bed, propped up on one elbow. Jane eased her legs over the side and sat straight up.

She raised arms to attend her riot of black hair, running fingers through it, shaking, combing. This lifted her breasts. He did not move a muscle.

She stood and padded away from him, finding her work dress, bending at the waist to retrieve it between two fingers, then returning to full height, stretching to make her diminutive frame long.

"Nothing under," he said.

"Okay."

She smiled faintly, pulled the garment over her head, and settled it in place.

She must pass close on the way outside to the facility. She dare not avoid. Her first three steps were graceful and proud. Undefended. He enfolded her body, lifted her off the floor, spun her half around, set her down. Her arms around his neck gripped tight. Deep embrace for seconds. Not a word passed between. They did not kiss.

Jane unwound and glided out the side door.

Soon it was a grand breakfast. She shone with pleasure, making it. Exquisite butter and new bread took center place on their rough-hewn table, with the sound of frying and the smell of coffee everywhere. The eggs were fresh and discussing them opened questions.

"Miss Heather and Jacob?"

"Yep. I set aside a dozen-and-a-half for me for the week. The rest they take away, we split the sales. That plan is working."

"Did Jacob fix the bath heater?"

"Yes. He's young, but he's handy. Let's look at the list we gave him five weeks ago."

"Not yet."

"Okay." Jane resumed her enjoyment of golden eggs, bacon, bread, jam, and coffee. "Everything tastes so beautiful," she said with a glint in her voice.

"That is from finishing." One of their favorite words for it.

She colored, yet did not slow her fork.

"So, they work with you Tuesday, stay over in the bunkhouse, and then you all work together Wednesday?"

"Yes. I keep cooking! They are hungry. I send them off Wednesday after five o'clock dinner and they make it back home well before dark."

"Heather?"

"You know how I hate the iron? I truly hate it. We wash a week's clothes together Tuesday morning and Heather does the ironing. I could kiss her."

"Good. Are they ... 'happy'?" he asked, with a look.

"Oh yes oh yes they are so happy," she said. "On the way to the bunkhouse at night so happy and when they come in next morning so happy."

"Happy."

"Happy."

"Good for them," he said.

"All your clothes are clean and pressed and folded since four weeks, waiting for you."

"What about the five dollars?"

"They treasure the five dollars."

"Maybe it is too much."

"Maybe it's too little." Jane turned serious. "He only makes a few other dollars over the weekend shoeing for his uncle. That man pays Jacob too little." She pushed away from the table and gathered his rode-in clothes, plus a few items from his saddle bags, and set them to soak for washing.

Later they stood outside by the sizable porcelain bathtub with heating apparatus – a dangerous-looking contraption, vaguely reminiscent of a still. A cord of kindling and firewood lay near in a depression lower than the tub. Jane lit a fire beneath a tank on the device and began directing water into it. Another faucet began filling the tub from the reservoir.

"It'll take almost an hour to get just right hot," Jane said as the tub filled. "Jacob had to change the tubes, they weren't low enough. But now this really works."

They walked the yard, checking fences and the chicken coop, visiting the small barn and its two-section pasture sufficient for one cow and their two horses with grass watered from the well in seasons rain failed. The Jersey showed signs of recognizing him, greeting him home. Stopping by the garden, Jane poured out her ambitions for the coming spring. They included a second railing to support snow peas she liked, but which ran out too soon last summer. They sat on a stump and went over the fix list, many items of which had 'Jacob' printed next to them, adding a few things, celebrating the cross-out of others.

They ran out of topics. Jane stood and swayed away just enough. A fine breeze came up and disturbed her hair. The dress pressed against her hip. Her calm happiness prevailed, but threading through – a subtle restlessness, a delicious ache teasing to be noticed. She kept her body turned half-away from him.

The ache grew. She could not disguise it. She turned to face him, eye to eye, to show it. A beat of time – she turned and ran. Her head start was just enough to reach the bathtub first. She dove in with a squeal of shock and delight. Only two seconds to thrill to the perfect temperature – his arm shot under and around her waist to take her weight in control and lift her bodily out into his grasp, limbs flailing away. She unleashed her favorite screaming.

"No no no no no no no."

This time the dress did not survive. He ripped the drenched thing off her body and threw it aside. He spun her and pushed her shiny-wet torso into the grass alongside the bath. One shin pinned her down at her low back. He yanked her legs one at a time into bent position, folding knees up and under, which raised her bottom high in the air.

"I am not an animal," she sobbed.

"We both are."

The sound of his pants coming off caused a jolt in her gut. She flailed one arm behind to fend off – he grabbed the wrist and shoved it to the earth. He removed his leg from her back, swiveled behind, and forced her thighs apart.

The cock drove deep.

"Na yi yi yi oh fucking no."

Feet flat on the ground outside her knees, crouching to stay well-aimed, he found his stroke. Nothing impeded it. He tangled his left hand in her wet hair and pulled back, slid the other hand around her neck.

With strong hands controlling her head and an erect phallus slamming home like the piston of an engine – pinned down and helpless – delicious fright rose like a demon in her belly.

"Whorooh ..." her terror rushed out.

Her knees ground into the grass. His hands keep her head bent back, his strength forced her breasts against the earth. Relentless strokes grew enormous with his power.

"Na. Yi. No. No. Whum. Wha. Na."

Jane shifted hips with each thrust. Not to avoid – to

make the splendid rod touch her pleasure best. She wiggled into it.

"Greedy," he grunted.

"Fuck me fuck me fuck me. Right there. There. There."

"Greedy."

Their bodies reached unity, slicked in juices, thrusting, squeezing, grunting as breaths exploded.

He stopped. Cock pulled out. "Open."

Jane obeyed. Each hand came from under and reached behind to rest on the mounds. Fingers slipped into place. One from each hand curled along the outer lips. In one graceful flow, her left leg slid to the side with his thigh pushing it, her back arched another inch of angle, and the fingers pulled the glistening sex wide.

The rod thrust hard. It rippled through vagina with the sound of mud sucking wet.

"Oh hrummm..." she grunted, and then a huge breath ... "Fuck!"

He pulled out. Thrust in again.

"Fuck!" Her fingers stayed at the rim to feel the rush of flesh penetrating her time after time. She grunted the air out of her body with each.

"Hunh. Hunh. Fuck. Hunh. Hunh."

He stayed in a crouch, removed hands from her hair and neck, and straightened upright from the waist. Leverage came from strong legs pushing off the earth. His thrusts accelerated. He began to yell, "Yi. Yi. Yi." The louder with each, the closer to his ride-home he rode.

"Ya. Ya. Ya. Ya." His arms rose with each shout, reaching up, up.

With penetrations deep to touch her cervix, Jane lusted for cock to break into her womb, and more, all into

her melted body, all past her belly, up between her
breasts, yes, to have the fucking thing slam into her heart.
She prayed he would thrust into the sky a million times,
with a woman's vagina to catch it. She seemed
transparent, so perfectly did her body take him in. His
final brutal penetrations went home. He bellowed.

"Oh. Yes. Oh. Ha. Ha ..." then screamed to bursting
... "Ha!"

She swiveled below, subtly, to get the spurting all
around inside – his third spurting in four hours of this
wild day. Some clenching told of her own quiet
explosion. It filled her pelvis with hot radiance. She did
not cry out to let him know about that.

He yanked himself out to stand proud. Wet glistened
on the triumphant organ. Looking out to the horizon, he
froze as if in victory over a great beast. Then he seemed to
notice a woman melted around his legs. He picked her up
and settled her into the bathtub. Grass and dirt flushed
away from her body into the water.

He strode away, naked, to check on his horse.

Jane clung to the side of the tub to keep from slipping
under the water, helpless with joy.

~~~~~

They luxuriated in the bath.

The heater was working wonderfully, the afternoon
was bright, their world was under control. Two bodies
floated in a pool of happiness much richer than
bathwater. She lay propped up against him, between his
legs, with her back to him.

"Who said you could do that to me?" she asked.

"You did."

"I'm sad for my poor dress."

"You do not sound too sad."

"It's hard to show my tragic sorrow right now."

"Heh."

"Anyway, it was just a garden-work rag. Threadbare. I could have pulled it off before you grabbed me, but I wanted you to rip it off. A grand ending for that dress."

"You."

"What?"

"You, Jane. You said I could."

They paused. Her hand swayed in the water making ripples that ran back against the tiny ones from the west wind flowing over the homestead. She did not spin to look in his eyes. She closed hers.

They welcomed exchanging consent, especially when separated for weeks. Now, the renewal.

"Take me like that. Whenever you want. Just put me down and take me."

"My duty as the man."

Jane laughed well over that. Now she rotated in the tub, her torso fronting his. A film of sweat caused by the hot water made his skin glisten. The stubble-beard shone stark black and shiny. As always, she treasured the story of competing heritage in his rough features.

"It's a thrill to feel you slam in and send the male power right up my spine."

His eyes closed. He drew a breath and held. Her words had pierced his heart – she was proud of them. She did not resume for many seconds.

"I have my 'stop,' but I don't use it hardly ever."

"No, you do not." His eyes opened. "But you have it."

"Yes."

The emotions of risk flickered between. The emotions

of trust, as well. She waited for them to settle.

"Put your power on me."

He nodded. Their gaze held solid.

She said, "I've been thinking about it. Men just take without asking. And there's no 'stop'."

"Yes," he said. "Many. Some."

"That's the way of it."

"It is not right, Jane."

"I can speak up. Those other men would slap their women down for trying to talk about it. Or if she needs to say 'stop.' It rages me women cannot make it 'stop'."

"Yes. It is wrong."

"They'd mock you for being a gelding instead of a stallion if they found out I can say 'stop'."

"They are stupid animals, rutting just to spurt it out. I am glad 'stop' means 'stop.' And I am really glad 'no' means 'keep going'."

"Yes! Yes! Oh, oh oh oh never take my 'no' away. I can't live without it. No no no no no."

"You want it, Jane. On your own. You want pleasure to be taken. Hard."

"Yes. I want it. I ache for it."

"That is what makes me slam in like that."

"Because I'm giving my body?"

"Yes. You give it freely and we fuck you together."

"Oh ..." It made her suck in her breath. They froze, letting it set in. "Say it again."

"You give your body, and we ravage it together."

A shudder ran through her frame. "I do give my body."

Jane felt his erection bloom against her belly. She put her hand on it.

"I'll never get over ... you get hard so easy. All these

two years. The thing is always doing this."

"If we did something about it every time, the cow would never get milked."

Jane laughed with delight. "We'll hole up in the bedroom and I'll yell through the door for Heather to do everything. Slip five extra dollars under the sill for her to stay two more days. She'll be curious. I'll just scream out, 'he won't stop fucking me'."

~~~~~

This night, Jane wanted gentle. She did not have to say it – he knew. She settled clean sheets on the bed. She lit three candles and turned off the big oil lamp. She considered putting a drop of perfume behind her ear, but seeing him watching, she declined it – he was so beautiful, standing naked next to their bed, she believed her skin would bloom sweet on its own from his presence.

He was hers. Almost two years in, and still true – he belonged to her. She possessed her own cowboy. Just as exciting, he is the wild man who would catch her from behind if she tried to flee, throwing a lariat to bind her helpless. Because she belonged to him.

His face bore stubble, his eyes shone bright from claiming his place. Standing frozen in their little tableau, she savored the impression his hard body had thrust on her all day, from the moment he stormed up and jumped off his horse. He had bruised her body and soul – it was delicious – now she wanted gentle.

She moved slowly to the bed, watching him watch her naked body. Arriving, she circled his neck with eager arms, pressed her breasts to his chest, and softened inside out when his hands on her back and hips pulled tight to complete the embrace.

They stood by the bed and kissed.

She held still to let his mouth roam hers, turning her head to abet his tongue touching where it willed. To let their liquids gather – not to swallow, rather to bathe in the erotic taste and feel of it. With no hurry, awareness of their bare bodies widened. She swayed her torso gently, slipping back and forth on his, and pressed back when he asserted his dangerous pelvis against hers.

Should she signal him to act – to invite the masterful taking? Instead, and she kept her kissing subtle – to hold the storm in abeyance.

They pulled apart.

"Who told you you could kiss me that deep?"

"You did, Jane."

"Deeper," she said.

The next kiss thrilled. He slipped in further than ever. She squirmed to show her hunger for it. He sensed it, and his organ swelled against her belly. Jane let the kiss endure for seconds, minutes – his mouth buried deep, deep in hers.

Finally, she pulled back. With a glance into his eyes, she eased her body down his, kneeling at his feet. She guided his organ to her lips and slipped it into her mouth.

The shape of it. The thickness, heft. The awareness of how rudely it penetrates, this thing so alive in her mouth, which violates with frightening power – it had fucked her into the ground a few hours past. She contained it, warming to the surety of her control, yet ready should he shake off her gentle engulfment. She slid off.

"Take over," she said. Not meaning it.

"No. Do it for three hours."

"I love it in my mouth."

"Four hours."

She moved her hand away from the shaft and looked up into his eyes.

"Slide it in. I'll hold steady. Be gentle. But slide in."

Her hands rested on his thighs. He brought the tip to her lips. They made a bond of eyes. She held herself rock steady.

The shaft slipped in. There came a beautiful sound of wetness pushed asunder.

In – hold – stay locked with eyes – slide out – slow. Again. Again. Again.

Her head moved with great delicacy to make each half-deep penetration smooth. She breathed around him. The inside juice of her mouth began to overflow. Some fell onto her chest and trailed across one breast.

He pulled back.

"... right in you."

"So beautiful. I love it in my mouth. Don't stop."

"Right in your mouth."

"Yes. Don't stop."

His rhythm resumed. Still gentle, but quicker. Again. Again. Again.

A spark in her eyes said he could go deeper. Jane sent the wish, while fighting the urge to lunge forward on the next stroke and force it. When he slowed, the intent shone clear in his eyes. Very simply, very softly, he eased forward, made the cock pause at the opening at the back of her mouth, and gently pushed through. The shaft penetrated to its base.

"Agggg..."

He pulled out fast. Her eyes teared over and she gasped for air and safety. Five weeks no practice – she had lost the knack. But then she tilted her eyes to his and nodded. He carefully lowered himself to the root in her again.

She accepted the phallus deep many times. With each, tolerance for it grew, until she could abide it sliding all the way into her throat with no alarm, no physical rejection, no panic.

So vulgar an act, made sacred by their courageous intimacy of heart, unafraid of sin – her throat had become the organ to catch his thrusts into the sky.

She removed her hands from his thighs, eased them behind her body and clasped them together. She sank lower and tilted her head to keep his aim true. Her breasts, glistening, pointed up. The supplication in it nearly sent him off. He slithered deep into this new girl.

"Oh Lord," he said.

His stroke slowed, else the next one would be the last. Jane wanted it, yet she put her lust on pause. She eased him out. "Not yet," she whispered. "But when it's time, I'll drink it all."

His eyes closed and he took two deep breaths. Jane rose. She took his hand in hers, like a girl saying *yes* to a man courting her. She stood rock steady. His eyes opened and fixed solid on her mouth, a wet mouth with lips swollen. She parted them slightly.

Jane sank into a dream. She felt the beats change, one by one – she was his mistress, then his shy wife, then a debased harlot, then an angel whispering of her purity during sex. His eyes remained on her mouth. She parted lips more. Liquid trailed onto her body. She did not hinder this, tilted to let more flow.

"Everyone thinks I got myself a nice country woman hidden somewhere."

"Yes."

"Sweet and gentle and pure."

"Yes."

"Obedient and hard working."

"Yes."

"They do not know about her down in the mud begging for another one."

Jane did not speak –*proud to be that woman*. She let both her goodness and her greed for cock shine in her eyes. Deliberately, she turned her head slowly to face him square, and opened her mouth. All the insides were wet and pink-swollen. She let him look. She let softness blossom, in her jaw, her lips, her throat. A shudder said he could sense it.

She led him two steps to the bed and gestured for him to lie there. Her body slid on top. She took the cock in hand and slipped down until her breasts rested on it. She let their softness cradle and caress. She looked up.

"Just let me."

He nodded. He stretched his hands above his head to grasp the rails of the bedstead.

She was alone with it, then. Her hair fell around, onto his groin, and she was alone inside. The desire to send pleasure swelled, yet also the urge to be penetrated. She held both in her heart. Her lips separated. Her hand around the shaft tilted the tip right in. She lowered with grace, flesh on flesh, smoothly, pausing at the first limit, then surrendering and expanding her arousal to accept all – her descent forcing the tip all the way to the back of her throat, past the narrowness, and another inch embedded into the openness.

He groaned with sweet agony. She did not pull back, instead contracting and releasing pressure around him in a rhythmic pulse. Magnificent wetness filled her mouth.

She swayed in it. Wait, wait, another pulse, she pressed even deeper, as if cock could never find anything to stop it, wanting it to try, gurgling with the effort to slip it deep, deep, deep.

Even then, Jane was all accommodating. There was no panic. Even as she withdrew, there was no escape-intent, only the longing for adieu, tempered with knowing she would make the impalement again, soon, again, soon, again.

Twice more, each time slower, Jane made the raging-hard erection slide deep. She marveled he did not erupt, with erotic heat flooding the nexus, with his wild drives surely provoked. She was ready. She would accept. But he did not.

Then, with the tip outside her lips, reality switched: it was not her mouth an inch away, it was her sex. She believed with certainty these lips were those between her legs – they were now tender labia. When the opening grew, it was the gate of vagina. With heart bursting, she lowered her mouth-cunt onto the phallus that loved it so.

She impaled herself on it with wantonness. The illusion swelled. The more she lowered her mouth on him, the hotter transformed reality grew.

Suddenly, the illusion shattered. She pulled off, jerked her head up to look in his eyes, rose up wild with lust and swung her legs around his body, released her hips to let cock penetrate true. They screamed with delight and excitement.

Jane stayed in a crouch, feet flat on the bed on either side of his hips, both hands on his chest. Her long dance began, swaying, squeezing, lifting, settling, occasionally letting her weight down fully to see how deep she could get the rod jammed up inside. She would not let him thrust, saying 'no' to it once. She only wanted hard cock, immortally rigid forever, frozen, with which to ravage her sex. Her breasts quivered and her breath raced as she let her arousal run free. With increasing speed and abandon, she vaulted up, knowing his body would not fail. She reached the top, slowing her hips, putting power into three enormous engulfments.

"Yes. Yes. Yessss...." she screamed.

An explosion of liquids, a seizure of every limb, and wild exclamations of joy – the bursting was full of amazement, laughter, and release. She squeezed muscles to set the pleasure deep – yet they trembled with excitement uncontrolled. She looked in his eyes at times while savoring her body's abandon. He cooed a word or two of carnal endearments, which made her blush and nod her head.

There was wet everywhere.

Then, a moment along her satisfaction – she saw yearning in his eyes – Jane sobered greatly, slipped off the mighty prong, and slowly, with deliberate sensation, shifted down his body. Her breasts became wet with her juice on his belly.

She arrived below. She looked up at him. Her eyes were dark with passion when she spoke.

"Spill it in my mouth."

~~~~~

The jangle woke her.

She jerked upright. He was dressing in his clean range clothes. The spurs spinning as he pulled on his boots broke her heart. She began to weep.

"No."

"I have to. Day and a night riding here, day and a night in bed with you, two days back, and greenhorn cowboys riding the herd. Peterson deserted me."

"What?"

"I have no foreman now. He took a sack of flour, a bottle of whiskey, some bullets, and rode off in the night. I have no foreman."

She stood up, naked, unashamed of her tears.

"William Bennis Hovey."

He stopped dressing. The sharp call of his full name – he froze in respect.

"Get back in this bed."

"No, Jane."

"Cruel cruel cruel."

"My fortune is in that herd, we agreed to this plan, I risked coming here anyway, at the worst moment. It might be a long time –"

"I'm coming with you."

"You know the reasons why not."

"You are more cruel than the land."

She ran across, threw herself against him, pouring out rage against fate. He bent her into his body and overwhelmed her with a gigantic kiss.

He wrenched them apart.

"Every day as the sun sets," he said, "I will put my mind on you, on your body and its wicked tricks. You do the same, Jane. At sunset."

"No."

"Yes."

She quieted her heaving breast. She pulled back tears. Their eyes held each other in power to keep heaven with hell all around.

"I will," she whispered.

William Hovey picked up his saddle bags, turned and strode out to his horse in the dawn light, spurs singing their tingling song, every step kicking up dust to the wind.

~~~~~

The echoes of his departure subsided.

Jane stood rigid in the doorway. The wind blew against her nakedness.

Everyone else in the world would advise her to shrug it off, get busy. No. The pain would not fade today. She was determined to let it hurt all the way down. She would rather have railed against his will, fought like a she-puma until they began gentling with salacious sex. Instead, he rode away with half.

She could coast. Heather and Jacob would not arrive until tomorrow. No washing, no planting, no woodcutting, no labor today. She only had to milk the cow and throw some corn to the chickens, which might be accomplished in a daze.

After minutes at the door with focus on the exact spot Hovey crossed out of sight between the two hills to the west, she turned inward, entertaining a healthy rage in her chest. She strode to her clothing alcove. She visited each garment hanging there, finally easing a plain cotton sun dress out, lifting it over her head to settle it down her body.

Her eye caught on a fancy box in the farthest corner of the closet. She stared at it.

"An evil thing," she mumbled.

She pulled the thing from its place, turned to sit on the edge of the bed. To remove the lid of the thing might spark something happy. The box radiated it.

   She suppressed the urge.

   "... not yet," she spit out the window after him.

   Instead, while the sun burst upon a fine April morning across the American West, she remained sitting on the bed, but cast her mind back nearly two years, recalling the cause of all trouble – the waking of her astonishing libido.

part 2
july-august 1895

beautiful-strange

j.j.kirnan

July 21, 1895
Sunday
Silver City, New Mexico

The rain stopped. The water did not.

The flood reached a peak in the middle of the night. The flash carved a huge ditch straight down Main Street. It washed out a score of businesses, including the feed store of Jane's uncle, and with it her bedroom and most of her belongings brought to this town from the East two years prior. Her second tragedy in two years.

At dawn, Jane sat numb on the back porch of a Bullard Street hotel, which had narrowly survived – there was a river in its backyard now. Her aunt sat nearby, sullen and defeated, with dried-up eyes. Her uncle gave out the fated news.

"We're leaving, Jane. East. Back to New York, to the lake country there. To Ithaca. We should never have left."

"When?"

"Right away."

"Oh."

"Jane, come along."

No. She would not. Could not. East held only pain – her obstinacy would endure to defy it. She held forth against their pleading for an hour, until they surrendered. Then, her aunt told the secret.

"We have a property here, Jane. We haven't been out there for three years. A little ranch, seven miles west. We are not homesteaders. We got it in exchange for a grub stake for three wildcat miners. It's miserable, I'm sure. Deserted and dried up. Or washed away."

The next day, Jane bade farewell to the couple. Her
uncle willed his last few things that would not go on the
train – a grey gelding, its saddle and gear, a few pieces of
gold. And the deed to the ranch, signed over legal this
very day, her nineteenth birthday, Tuesday July 23, 1895.

Jane traded with the hotel, washing work for staff
meals and a tiny maid's room at the side. She gave one
piece of silver to the livery next door to board the horse
for a month. In the uproar of a ruined town, and cascades
of more rain, Jane turned inward, diminishing, unable
even to hate the dangerous new river rushing by where
once her life seemed safe.

July 27, 1895
Saturday
Bullard Street, Silver City, New Mexico

At dawn, a week after the flood, Jane threw open her
window and confirmed the end of something – bright
sun on wet earth and a turn in the direction of the wind.
Yet despondent loneliness set about her shoulders. She
wished to not throw it off.

Next door, across a thirty-foot-wide yard – someone
new. He turned out of the side entrance of the livery
stable and came to a halt at its outside wash basin. Naked
from the waist up. Dark brown hair flowing, thick on his
head, luxurious on his wide chest. Strong, lifting a large
rainwater basin above, pouring it over, not caring if his
trousers soaked.

"Yaaah ..." he cried, with a shudder to fend off the
cold.

Jane watched him wash. She watched him shave. She

watched his body move, slender yet sturdy from inside out. His face – beautiful-strange, a man animal of primitive heritage jumbled in the New Mexico mix. Skin browned by the sun covered tough sinew and muscle. A pale scar ran across his abdomen and up his left side.

Her desolation seized tight – a wordless purpose surrounded it in an instant. Moving slowly, she floated to the door of her room and eased outside. Unnoticed. Ten steps, carefully chosen, to circle into his side vision. He paused drying his hair.

Jane approached, graceful as if in ritual. She stopped before him. All waited.

Her hand lifted in an arc. She placed the palm square on his chest. He remained solidly in place, unblinking and severe.

The world would allow this. Would let neither quail. Would defy the normal to intrude. Would expand their fixed gaze to grow magnificent and wide, with her wounded heart exposed and the beauty of it flowing down her arm, into her fingers, into him.

"I am virgin," she said.

He nodded.

A bellow from inside the building.

"Hovey!"

He did not startle. For a second, their eyes held.

Then he turned away and disappeared.

~~~~~

Jane asked to work extra this day, Saturday, to not work the next, Sunday. She set to the hotel's laundry with furious intent. She refused to look outside. At dusk she stumbled to her room, threw off her clothes and sank into bed. As the sounds of work paused in the adjacent kitchen and laundry, her strength waxed steadily, until enough to throw on a robe and slip into the nearby bathroom.

Jane washed. Twice. There was a huge mirror in the bath, seeming to tease her to look.

If anyone thought her plain, they would miss the demure slight slenderness, the oval of hips so woman-true, with the delta centered and inviting, and sweet breasts in proportion, up-tilted. Erect carriage stood her proud with no effort.

She was glad to be thought plain of face, to hide.

Jane slipped into the robe and padded to her room. Blissful – the fire in a potbelly stove, the crackle giving comfort as much as the heat. She paced, sat in a chair, flopped on the bed, fed the stove, sat again, and brushed her hair. Then, after an hour, she walked to the door, ascertained it was unlocked, and positioned herself with back to the wall near the front right corner. Her breathing steadied as the night grew. She took infinite possession of the floor beneath her feet, and the solid earth under it, which she also owned.

She heard no step. The door opened.

Hovey.

He closed the door and locked its mechanism. They stood ten feet apart, unmoving.

Jane felt her back against the wall. She liked having no escape. Except her will.

He approached.

Hovey's hand parted the top of her robe. Its palm came to rest on her chest, an echo of her gesture of the morning. She shuddered, then pressed forward into his hand and opened her eyes. For three breaths their understanding deepened. His eyes so dark it astounded there could be a glint in them like this, face so ragged it shocked how unafraid she felt.

He slipped his hand behind her waist and pulled her body in with strength, taking her mouth under his. Jane's arms circled his neck. He pressed her against the wall. They twisted in embrace, fighting like angels starving for pleasure. Jane craved his mouth on hers, yet it lasted only a few seconds. Hovey pushed her head aside and opened his mouth on her neck, then up under her chin, then down into the vee at the top of her breasts.

Then ... she shut down. She squirmed to the side. Something made him accept the pause. Her hand reached out, fit to the length of hardness pushing out the front of his breeches. She lifted her eyes to his.

"Yes," he said. The first word she heard him speak. "Do not tell me your name yet."

Jane nodded to agree. She unbuttoned. It sprung up and fell into her hand. She had no name for "it" but loved it anyway, forever, from that second.

The pants dropped to the ground and he stepped out of them.

"I stayed out on the trail too long. Your touch will set it off quick. This is the first thing."

Jane fit her hand around the shaft. She lowered into a crouch. So soft and so hard, so fearless and frightening. Moving the skin in rhythm over the inner firmness, it surely grew. With every stroke, the astonishment, *how can this go in me?*

"Yes, like that," he said.

From never having seen one in her life, to urging it to grand erection, Jane jumped in fast, varying speed and grip. The situation made her smile in dubious belief, so absurd, so dangerously ridiculous – her small hand inciting the 'mighty organ of manhood.'

Arousal simmered.

In utter fascination, Jane slid her hand along the shaft again and again. He began to rock in time to her rhythm. Then, with more urgency, to thrust into her grip. Now a grunt on each stroke.

"Hmpf, hunh, hunh, nah ..."

She squealed with excitement. "Ohhh ... oh ... oh ... Oh!"

A final rough jerk of his body, a spurt straight up, and her hand filled with spill – creamy, warm, abundant. Shocked, she kept sliding along the shaft, now covered and slick. She did not recoil from the viscid flood. Hovey's body shuddered. He moaned. She looked up into his eyes.

"A man's greatest achievement," she said, impudence in the corner of her smile.

He pulled away and fell onto the bed face up. His hand took over, pulling the juice up onto his belly, stroking the organ to finish his pleasure.

"This is what happens," he said, breathing hard between words. "It is good you see it."

She stood marveling at the organ in his hand. One last drop appeared at the tip. Without taking her eyes off it, her shiny hand rose near her mouth.

"This is the scent of a man?"

"Yes."

"I can still feel the kissing, and now this scent. Why did you kiss me?"

"To stir us up."

"A girl told me a woman just lays on her back, lets it happen, it's over in a few minutes, and that's all there is.

No kissing."

"That is not your fate."

"Why?"

"I want far more than that from a woman."

"What are you going to do to me?"

"Make you lust for it every day for the rest of your life."

Her dry hand clasped over her mouth.

"Every day," he said.

Hovey kept stroking himself.

"Take off the robe."

Jane froze. Her modesty had been shredded, with man-juice all over her hands to show for it, yet a reticence clung.

"No." She grabbed a towel nearby and cleaned her hands. She threw it at him.

"Instead, should I have you take it in your mouth until I explode again?"

She blushed hot-red.

"Yes," she blubbered. Joking. Looking at it.

"Come here." He wiped himself dry.

Jane pulled the robe tighter and sat on the edge of the bed. The scent of him surrounded. She wrapped her left hand around the cock.

"What's the best word for it?" she asked.

"Cock."

"Cock?"

"Yes."

Her eyes came up to his.

"I can't believe how much came out."

"I am a hunter. Stayed out on the trail too long."

"No woman for months?"

"A man can release, alone, out there. Not the same as

in a woman's body."

"Oh!" she said.

"You release, at night, by yourself."

Jane's eyes got big. "No, I don't. Never. Women don't."

"Tell the truth."

She shook her head, a little sadly. She stroked him. The astonishing cock.

"That feels fine, your hand on it after."

"Will it erupt like a volcano again now?"

"No."

"If you are a hunter, why are you in this town working at a livery stable?"

"The rains drove me in. And I will take civilization on times."

"Oh."

"... not the real reason."

"What is it?"

"This in this bed."

"You came in town to have a woman?"

"Yes."

"When?"

"Last evening."

"Did you go straight to the bordello?"

"No. I slept right through, until you saw me washing this morning."

"I slept through life until I saw you washing this morning."

Hovey's eyes closed. She stopped her hand. Stopped everything, until he opened his eyes and spoke.

"You are a woman who can say things like that?"

"My mother was smart. My father. They gave it to me. Words. Poetry."

"How old are you?"

"Nineteen."

"Why did you sleep?"

Jane let her truth well up. The emptiness.

"All my people died in one day last year, Hovey. In the East. All of them. And my life here got drowned a week ago. I lost precious letters and pictures. Nothing means anything to me, not even my hand on you like this. Nothing."

More pain in her face than even these dreadful words could say.

She removed her hand from the softening organ.

He shifted in the bed.

"No man has ever seen your body."

"No."

"It is private."

"Yes."

"Treasure your modesty. A pride of the virgin. Let it go only as you will."

Jane considered this surprising advice. She stood and walked near the door. She hovered as long as her nineteen years wanted. Then she let the robe drop to the floor – as if putting nakedness on, not taking something off. She took two steps toward Hovey, to show.

"Stay there," he said.

His eyes knew no reluctance. Jane followed their searching, each passing second raising a new pride, to make a man look. The cock stirred.

"Oh oh oh oh," One hand covered her mouth, eyes squinting with delight. She barely restrained herself jumping into bed to land on top of it. Instead, she swayed.

"Raise your arms high."

She did it slowly while twisting at the hips, could feel heat pouring off her breasts, saw he was caught by their offering.

"Turn around. Slow."

She bent arms at the elbow to let forearms rest on her head and used a step in the swaying to rotate. Facing away, she rose on toes, arched her back and lifted hands to the ceiling. Then, at an angle to his vision, her body bent into an s-shape. She lowered from her tiptoes until her feet were flat on the floor, yet the curving form remained.

"Around."

She spun and stopped.

"Why has no man sought you?"

"I am not pretty. I know how to hide in a room full of girls. I don't want it."

"You do not want it?"

She shook her head. *No want. No.*

"Why?"

"Heart like a dry well."

Hovey held his organ firm. His eyes narrowed.

"... finest body of any woman I have had."

Jane stared at him. "Have you had a hundred?"

"No. Only two – had. But more, visited for an hour."

"Did you marry the two?"

"No."

"How old are you?"

"Twenty-four."

Hovey rose from the bed and took her in his arms. A man's hands on her naked body – it stopped her breath. The touching claimed her surely, her back, her sides, and up under her hair at her neck. While she was naked.

A kiss erupted, amplified by the lusciousness of his flesh pressing hers, with the hard thing impatient against her belly. As before, he quickly pulled away from her mouth and trailed kisses down her neck, pushing her head to the side to take possession there.

Then his mouth reached her breasts. His lips surrounded the tips one at a time, sending flashes of excitement down her back.

"Kiss them, kiss them."

A man so intimate, devouring her body which had lived guarded so long – she thrilled with each new buzz, the quiver from giving herself away.

He straightened, tilted her head, and renewed the wild meeting of their mouths. Deep, thirsty, wet. His hand came to her throat and encircled, a light entrapment. She released any fear and let him. His hand swayed her neck to help his mouth find the deepest angle inside hers.

Too soon, he lifted her in his arms and set her on the bed. No matter what to follow, she could not remove her eyes from his mouth, shocked by the beauty of the brief kisses.

I will make you erupt in my hands forever if you kiss me like that in the night until dawn.

Hovey placed his hand on her chest once more.

"Before I enter you, tell me your name."

"I am Jane Cady Whitfield."

"Jane."

"I want your name to be only 'Hovey.' Don't tell me anything more. Hovey."

His hand moved to her belly. She shuddered under it. He waited until she settled.

"This is the next thing. To open. To offer."

Jane nodded.

"Do not look away."

She opened her thighs. Her breath came in gulps. She

fought the need to escape his gaze, to diminish the exposure that made her shiver. Again, he waited until she settled. Then, with surety of fate, his hand slipped down and fit the vee with perfection, taking the puffy mound in his palm, rocking with tenderness to cover.

"Oh oh oh." She slammed her legs shut. "Oh no oh no."

"Your man's hand belongs there."

"Oh."

Slowly, hesitating, she released. Thighs parted. In a moment she lay wide open and offered on the bed, thick with bittersweet vulnerability in her chest. His hand covered again.

"After this, if you agree to it, I will not ask, Jane Whitfield. I will touch when I want. Take when I want. Unless you say 'stop.' Or if you do not want me after tonight. But to take your virginity, now, you must say so."

"You can't take it. It is mine. I will never let anyone take it. But with you I end it. Now."

A flicker of surprise in his eyes. Her words made him hold for ten enormous seconds. Then, his hand began moving, pressing, sliding. Their gaze held, even when his fingers parted the halves of her sex, even when his touching roused the bud nestled at the top of the lips. He caressed in the wet.

Jane's hips moved to the rhythm of his hand. Her breath came quickly. She let each out with a sighing cry. Then she felt his fingers at the opening, riming it, carefully discovering the edge-line of her innocence and womanhood. She nodded to him.

"Yes. Yes."

One finger slipped in, finding resistance.

"It will hurt."

"... in me."

Then, Hovey was above, between her open thighs, torso supported on one arm, the other guiding the phallus. They held eyes, as she knew he wanted, even when the shaft eased forward and pushed past the barrier.

"Oh. Oh."

Hovey held still, halfway in. Jane's pelvis rotated to accommodate. They let her pain subside. In a moment, a small smile appeared on her face, and she lifted her arms from the bed to encircle his neck.

"Yes, Hovey, yes."

He drew out until the head emerged. Side to side movement, to enlarge the opening. Then gently, confidently, his body arched, weight eased forward – penetration to the bottom.

"Oh no oh oh oh," she cried. He held deep, pinning the certainty of it. "Oh oh oh."

Hovey made no sound. His body remained rock steady. She shifted under him, attempting to escape – and to wiggle onto the awful rod at the same time. In a moment, she settled, breath high in her chest, eyes still holding his.

"Yes," she whispered.

He drew out. Her stomach fell with an ache of loss – *ever to be filled again, ever to?* Then, the steady strokes began. Nothing existed except again.

Again. Again. Again.

She could barely breathe. To have a man between her legs, to feel him rocking. She increased the insistence of her arms around his neck, the invoking embrace. Her legs rose to surround his torso.

He pulled out and tilted her body on its left side.

Holding her right leg folded up and away, he entered from behind, so smooth, so good. His right hand could now angle perfectly to caress the little bud. He thrust again and again while caressing with fingers.

Turned away from his gaze, Jane fell into her own world. Hunger to have it put on her ... then desperate to leap up and flee ... then screaming inside to spin and pound his body with her fists.

Then – to surrender.

Her pelvis released, her thighs relaxed, her breath melted into serenity. Instantly, everything liquified ... *did he expend? No, my body!* Hovey's thrusts quickened with the flood. His fingers moved faster, now stroking deep around the gland, taking the flesh under them like cream coming to butter. She ceased to know the difference, the hand, the cock. Neither would stop. *He will not stop.*

Again. Again.

For the first time, Jane contracted her muscles around. They joined rhythms. Each stroke was theirs, together. They ascended. She felt a height approach – a startling destination, hidden until the moment of womanhood.

"Oh no. Oh no. Ya. Ya. Ya."

In a blinding flash she burst to the top. Her body arched, driving back against him. Her free leg thrust out, jerking and flailing. She grabbed a pillow and jammed it to her face. All turned to fire in her belly, her loins, and rushed wild through the flesh of her sex.

She screamed into the pillow.

A mighty contraction of every muscle.

She screamed again.

With a final thrust, Hovey drove deep, pinning her quivering body to the bed. Jane sputtered unknown cries into the pillow, wet with tears of impossible wonder.

~~~~~

"You didn't let go in me," she said.

"Do not need to, every time."

"Oh."

"I like being hard, being in."

"Oh."

"To have a woman explode in my bed."

"Oh. Oh. It *was* like an explosion. I didn't know."

"You gave yourself not married," he said.

"I will never marry."

"Nor I."

They lay side by side in her small bed, facing. His words had come after minutes of coasting in silence. The silence of her first *after*.

"What do we call this?" she asked.

"Fucking."

"No, oh not that word."

"Fucking."

"Hovey, it's ugly. Dirty and ugly. Hateful. People scream it at each other to hurt."

"There is no better word."

She took a deep breath. "Will that ... erupting ... happen to me every time? What do you call it?"

"Call it 'finishing'."

For a moment, Jane could not speak. The surprise of finishing had laid her low. Her body weighed nothing – and four hundred pounds. She absurdly believed such languor might not permit rising from her position half-wrapped around him. There was pain between the lips of her sex – which drew attention to its happy drama. Her mouth wanted kisses, that registered a little. Except for short kisses, he had avoided her mouth with his.

"Do all the women in this town finish?"

"No."

"Do the girls in Miss Honeyhurst's?" The only bordello in town.

"Never."

"I don't understand. It's heaven in a bed. I can barely move right now. I feel like bread pudding. You rightly finished me off, Hovey."

"I knew I could. I knew you could."

"How?"

Hovey told her a story, in his sentences of few words. How Marguerite, the owner of a hotel in Laredo, Texas, took him to her bed and taught him – out of all the other young men that visited – how to satisfy a woman. How to care enough to do it. He was sixteen years old. Randy as a stallion, even then.

"She did it for the women, not for me."

"But you must have done something that made her choose you, teach you."

Hovey paused. Then, a rare smile.

"I finished her very fine the first night."

Jane laughed with delight. "At sixteen? No wonder she grabbed you tight."

"I believe I took to the task. She screamed like you just did."

"Well, I am dumb, because if all the ladies are not turning into bread pudding, something is wrong in the world. It's something grand."

"I thought you were dry and empty."

Dead silence. Jane lay still, floating in the sweet, yet the weight of the world crept up her spine.

"You put something hard in me and made me melt and scream and now I am all creamy and well finished." Delirious. "But I still have nothing in my heart."

She sat up, knees bent and arms wrapped around her shins. The sound of water returned, the new stream rushing past in the night, the flood that drowned her small comfort in Silver City. Now Jane told her story.

How two years ago, in December 1893, when she was seventeen, an epidemic swept through the town of Ithaca in New York state, killing over one hundred people, including many students and faculty of Cornell University. It entered Jane's home. The first to die was her father, a professor at the University.

"My mother, Virginia, held him in her arms. His agony was bad. She told me to leave the room. I refused. My father died in the morning, with his son moaning and crying loud in the next room. She was near exhaustion herself, but departed the dead body of her husband and stumbled over. My brother shook and bled for two hours. His bed was full of filth. He was dead at noon. Virginia looked at me with blank eyes, broken heart. She said 'Jane, I am already in hell.' I held her and kissed her and tried to shine my light into her, until her light went out."

Hovey said nothing.

"I sat in a chair and rocked for an hour. My dead family all around. Then I somehow walked down the street to the home of my best friend. Her mother came to the door. Angela died two hours before."

Jane sat frozen in place, filled with sorrow. When he did not leave the bed, she released, let the pain run full red in her chest.

"All my family died in one fucking day."

Still, he did not flinch. His hand moved, set itself on

her foot, its tenderness unleashing all. Jane heaved out her wretchedness and rage, snarling and weeping. The purge ran for five minutes. Hovey remained steadfast.

"I don't know why I am still alive."

Jane ran out of tears. She turned bitter eyes toward his.

"I should have been in college. But everything was ruined."

Hovey gave things time to settle. When her eyes dried up and she ended with a tremendous sigh, he spoke.

"So, I believe we cannot call it 'making love'."

"No." Utterly sober, Jane did not recognize irony. He kept going.

"Mating?"

"No."

"Shagging?"

"No."

"Poking?"

"No."

"You find the word, then."

"I'm nineteen years old naked in bed with a man he put it in me made me scream turned me into a puddle of cream even if I am empty inside I want to do only this for six years just like this."

"Yes."

"Do I have it right, you want me to have as much pleasure as you?"

"Yes."

"For a girl to finish like that?"

"Yes. A woman."

"Even though not one other man in New Mexico cares if a woman finishes?"

"Yes."

"It's not against the law?" She did not laugh.

"No."

Then a wan smile grew. "Apparently, I'm going to like being fucked!"

Hovey laughed. First time for that sound. Hovey laughing – it hurt and comforted.

"You are probably going to fuck me a lot now. Even if I am empty in my heart. I'm your sad in-town woman."

"Yes, Jane, I am going to fuck you."

They said the word back and forth many times – to wear it down, make it theirs with no ugly. It still had hardness to it. Cold. The world injected "fuck" with hurtful intent.

"Hovey? Wait ..."

"What?"

"Can we say 'pleasuring' sometimes? 'Please pleasure me'?"

He went silent. She remained seated with knees up, he lay prone at her feet. She waited.

"You didn't let go inside me," Jane said.

"No."

"Why?"

Hovey paused. "Do you like, it, the cock?"

Jane giggled. "You fucking bet I do."

"Right. But do not use the word too often, just enough."

"You're fucking right. I'll slow down using it."

"'Pleasuring' does not work as well, does it?"

"No."

"You like it, Jane. Cock. Now you must love it. That is the next thing."

Somehow, she precisely understood. She nodded.

"Fetch a cloth."

She scrambled out of bed and returned and cleaned him. She laughed, while. There was blood on the sheet.

"Good thing I'm in control of the laundry," she said, pushing him off, yanking the sheet away and throwing another on the bed.

"Lay down – and not on your belly," she said.

Amused, Hovey obeyed his new woman.

She held the wild thing in her hand. *This is the world with a cock in it.* It knocked her sideways, the jarring surreality of her simple girl hand holding a man's stupendous prodigious outrageous hot cock. It pulsed. She knew he did that on purpose.

Another layer of modesty filled her mind – a chaste young woman ought never do what she would do now. She honored the shyness of it, let it fill her chest, still ragged from weeping.

I mustn't.

Then, with tenderness, she took the phallus in her mouth. It penetrated, pricking deep her woman's privacy.

Right away, she loved it. She loved cock in her mouth. She guided it with one hand and found the way to avoid her teeth and slid with the rhythm of sex and made her jaw relax and let the wetness grow.

And loved it.

If anyone looked in the window, they would have seen a man prone on the bed, with a naked woman curled next to him gently taking his sex into her mouth with all affection, arousal, and peace. The man did not thrust back. His arms stretched above his head on the bed. The woman rested her free hand on his hip, and with the other guided the erect, strong shaft into her mouth over and over again. Occasionally, he gave a word of guidance.

Jane tried little maneuvers, a few tight squeezes, and

finally used hand and mouth together to urge the excitement on.

The urgency began. Jane quickened. She let the cock in deeper. She contracted around it. So much wetness released from the tissues of her mouth, the sound of it sloshing filled the room.

With a bellow, Hovey arched into her strokes. Jane felt the thing contract, then release. Her instinct knew to keep the back of her throat blocked, to accept his eruption – one impetuous spurt, then another, then two more, quick. She held solid for the shuddering final emptying, then gradually opened her throat, and little by little let the fluid flow back and down.

She caressed the shaft with her lips, drawing the last of his pleasure out, the last of his juice in, swallowing all.

July 28, 1895
Sunday
Seven miles east of Silver City

The first notice of the place was the motionless windmill. As Jane rounded a spur, the water reservoir came into view. Then, the ranch house, facing south. The place was not washed away, at least, with two perimeters of broken fencing and a small bunkhouse to the east side. All seemed dreary, like a ghostly destination abandoned by the spirits.

She had reached the place by mid-morning, a seven-mile ride along the slowly drying divide at the base of the Pinos Altos Range, having retrieved her grey gelding from the livery stable with no contact with the person she wished to avoid. Him.

Hovey had departed Jane's room soon after her splendid oral worship of his organ. She sat stunned on the side of the bed while he dressed. He addressed her stony silence.

"It would be wrong for me to sleep in your bed. But this night should not mean anything more or less that I am leaving."

"Cruel."

"No, Jane, you must be alone with your new life until dawn."

"Did Marguerite tell you that's what women want? Right after?"

"No."

She held him motionless with her eyes for seconds.

"If this was the only time, you will feel my wrath."

Hovey nodded grimly and walked out.

Now, she dismounted Grey and tethered him to a fence post. Passing through the failing fences, she approached the house across the dirt front yard. No glass in place. Door ajar. Planks missing from the front porch. Jane passed inside, a visitor. Ten minutes later she emerged – the owner.

Possession meant little without water – she stood at the base of the empty wooden reservoir, the windmill towering above. No parts of the mechanism appeared broken or rusted, although some elements were disassembled. It could not be assessed this day. She turned her back on it and took three steps.

And froze.

Nineteen. To own – what does that mean in these shoes? To possess dust. To put a falling-apart house right. To make water flow. To grow something. The wind stirred the dirt around her boots. A New Mexico July

monsoon approached from the west, beyond two hills –
she would need to race it to town. She took one step.

And froze again.

Once, twice, muscles in her pelvis contracted.

"Oh," she whispered to the wind.

Then, Jane ran.

~~~~~

Grey needed no urging. He raced down Bullard Street
in the barn stretch, horse and rider nearly invisible in the
deluge, and charged though the open front of the livery,
carrying rain and mud onto the tamped earthen floor.

Hovey wrapped his right arm around Jane's waist and
pulled her off. With his other, he stripped the bridle from
Grey. Jane spun out of his grasp and in three seconds un-
cinched the saddle, pulled it off, and slapped the horse
forward to his waiting stall.

They crashed together. Hovey lifted her, spun her,
and thrust her against a wall. She tried to kiss his mouth.
He avoided.

He took her wrists in his hands, yanked them high
above her head and against the wall. Her eyes sparked
defiance. He glared back.

"Your flow."

Jane shook, surprised. But she knew.

"Five days away."

Hovey nodded.

She spat it right on him. "You won't put a baby in me
today."

Hovey took his hands off her wrists.

"You are bound."

She jerked her arms down, shoved them against his

chest. He grasped them together and clamped them high on the wall again. "Accept it."

She should spit in his face. Instead, she swallowed the outside of her pride and tucked away her profound power. Hovey saw the release and dropped his hands. Jane struggled to fight him, but failed, constrained by the imaginary rope, She tried to kiss for revenge. He avoided.

Hovey pulled open three buttons of her riding skirt. It fell to the ground. He yanked down her undergarment. Jane twisted against the invisible bonds as he opened his trousers.

In one powerful rush, he crushed against her, forced her thighs wide with his, ran the underside of the hard organ down the waiting lips, then up, tilted, and thrust inside.

"Fuck," Jane screamed. "Fuck!"

He pulled back ... and rammed forward.

"Fuck!"

"Quiet"

"Cut the binding. I'll scratch your eyes out."

"You are bound."

Jane took the shocking jolts of weight and power forcing cock into her body.

Thrusting. Thrusting.

Now she tilted and swayed hips to guide his aim into her sex – an insolent act to spite control. He answered – three gigantic thrusts so deep the tip prodded her cervix.

If not for the flood in vagina, the attack would have burned her flesh. She ached to bring her hands down. It hurt her heart to be tied. Yet the secret indulgence of accepting power ran through. Then, a surge of rebellion. Arrogance to be bound – to be fucked against a wall. She would not finish this time. Did not want.

"... you caught a sweet virgin," she whispered.

Two thumping strokes on the edge of cruelty.

"Now fuck her."

"Rmmmrh. Rmn. Mrmm."

"Rude between her legs."

"Hrugg."

"Right there. Fuck her. Hard. Fuck her."

His power escalated at the fiery words. Cock thrust with defiance now. Braying shouts slammed the walls.

Jane's pride swelled. Her heart melted with the phantastic femme being ravished, as if she were alive with her in one soul.

"... tender young body."

 "Huh. Huh..."

"Fuck her a thousand times."

"Yah. Ha. Huh ..." He reached the possible moment, thudding, thrusting, achieving. "... Huh. Ha. Yaaaa ..."

The first spurt – she offered a serene face to his wild visage, whispering small, "Give me. Spill me. Fuck me to heaven."

The final massive stroke forced her body up the wall, burning skin. She did not care. He held deep, convulsing, eased back, then pushed inside again with diminished weight. Jane remained steady, a limpid body, calm, with sparking eyes while pinned by a ram organ embedded in vagina, his finishing pleasure draining into her soft body.

Slowly, she brought her arms down and unbuttoned her soaking-wet shirt. Still impaled, she wiggled out of it and an under-camisole. Naked now, except for boots. Hovey watched through squinting eyes, heaving like a spent horse. With drama, she crossed her wrists, raised her arms again, fixed them high with imaginary bonds. It lifted her breasts to him.

"I'll just hang on this wall until you want to fuck me again."

~~~~~

"Last night I learned the taste of it. Now I know the feel of it."

"What?"

"Your juice flooding my womb."

"Womb of no babies."

She had wrenched away from him in the livery stable, grabbed her sodden clothes from the ground, slid off to the side entrance. It would be thirty feet to her bedroom door, through the torrents of July monsoon. Hovey watched.

"Blanket," he said, pointing.

She shook her head. She turned a coquette's smile on him. "Tie me for real next time."

She ran out, across, heedless of rain or sordid eyes of others, squealing when thunder cracked overhead. While she washed and dried herself, he saw to Grey before joining her.

Now they lay in her bed, near the potbelly with a cherry-red glow in one spot. The rain continued.

"Hovey, I almost said 'stop' in the livery."

"When?"

"Right when you pushed me against the wall. I almost said 'stop.' Now I'm vexed I let you take me so hard. Tie me and take me brutal. Not even one day after my first sex. I let you."

"Why did you let me, Jane Witfield?"

"I made fear wait outside. To try you. The wild hunter from the wild."

He nodded.

"To be taken can be good?" she asked.

"It is in us. We are animals. The world is harsh. We want to possess."

Jane did not understand how her trust in Hovey arose. She felt her mother's heart nearby. She sighed.

"I liked it."

"I would have stopped."

They held eyes for a long minute.

"I want to finish now," Jane said.

"In an hour."

"No, Hovey, another way."

He did not speak. She touched his body here and there. Her breasts pressed his hard torso, against the scar there. "You like having a naked girl lying next to you in bed, don't you."

"Yes."

Jane shifted her torso. Rocked. Her voice fell to the very edge of silence ... "They are soft."

Hovey closed his eyes. "Yes."

Jane pressed against him.

She brightened.

"May I ask for something?"

"Yes."

"Most cowboys don't let their woman ask, I bet."

"I am not a cowboy."

"Okay. Then ... I want kissing. So far, we haven't, really. You keep dodging away."

Hovey's eyes squinted.

"Is a hunter okay to kiss?" she asked.

He didn't move. She regretted.

"Oh. Sorry. I'm sorry I asked to kiss. Say 'no'."

"Be careful what you ask for."

Jane blinked. She searched his face.

If I gentle him, he might never slam me against a wall again. I crave the dreamy kiss. But oh oh oh, danger – I want to be taken hard, by a strong man.

She took his hand and guided it between her thighs.

"... your hand there. Touch gentle. Stir me. Kiss my mouth. Kiss me. Finish me, Hovey, with touching and kissing, just that."

For an answer, Hovey slipped off the bed. He opened the feed door of the stove and tossed in several pieces of firewood, then closed it tight. Jane came next to him. He turned to welcome her close.

Her hand lifted to the side of his face, and fingers explored his curious visage. It was not symmetrical – yet differences side to side harmonized, even if odd. Jane's fingers fit to his shape, long bones under taut flesh, a prominent jawline with but short beard-hairs bristling. His forehead, smooth. A dominating feature: high cheekbones with flat planes, canted at a severe angle. Jane padded them with fingertips. Some strain from a strange people caused them. Then her fingertips moved with lightest touch on his lips. She showed her hunger for them. Hovey did not avoid her whisper-soft touches on his face.

"I shaved before you rode up."

She removed her hands and leaned forward.

His head tilted, and hers. Mouths approached. She swayed delicately, lips parted. Neither closed eyes – the tease was in them.

They moved close, then away, then close. Jane felt the kiss, real as rain, in the ephemeral space between. Curving mouths seemed to form it round. Exciting. Then Hovey fell back away from her arms.

"Is your camisole dry?"

Startled, she spun around. It hung near the fire. She tested.

"Yes."

"Put it on."

"Why, Hovey? Don't you like me bare naked?"

"Distracting."

Jane giggled. She yanked the garment off its hooks and quickly slipped it over her head and down her body. Its hem fell just below her belly button. But the tease of the almost-kiss was destroyed. She leapt into his embrace. Fast as a young wildcat, she unleashed play on Hovey, kissing kissing kissing. But a girl's fun kisses – not deep. He took them and gave back.

Then it slowed. She opened her eyes to find his. He parted her mouth with his lips and eased in. The tip of his tongue touched hers.

Jane spun out of his arms. Her hand came to her mouth, eyes big with wonder.

"Really?"

He nodded. "Let me. Do not kiss back."

She returned to Hovey's embrace. He took her bottom lip between his and caressed. Then the top. His wet transferred. He teased her mouth open and brought the underside of her lips into play. Wet grew there. He slipped his mouth back and forth several times across hers, like painting, entirely slick and sweet with their liquids. She cooed nicely.

Hovey pulled back and looked in her eyes.

"Do not swallow."

"I won't."

Their heads tilted. He shaped his mouth to hers. It fit so beautifully. So softly. Neither resisted, neither imposed. Small swaying, sealed and sweet. Gradually, Hovey eased her lips apart again. Jane held quiet, with eyes closed, time flowing peacefully.

He slipped inside. His lips fit under hers now, and she might only follow his will as he opened her. At a perfect moment, his lips surrounded the tip of her tongue, held for a second, then slid forward to encircle and caress.

She shuddered from top to toenails. To escape this lushness – no, to bear it. She was sure her heart beat fast as a hummingbird's. She held her tongue offered. He slipped back, paused, and surrounded it again – gentle penetrations, slipping down on her, all liquids gathering and slicking. Hovey did not stop for many rhythms. He drew her tongue into his mouth – inside her mouth – again and again.

Hovey's right hand fit around her neck, collaring. Not to tighten, only to suggest he could. The other hand joined, making a circlet of touch like a choker, yet with no tightening. It was carnal adoration and possession. Jane melted in its intent.

His mouth continued roaming hers, seeking, licking, kissing the warm flesh, frequently returning to the provocative tongue, offered and taken with silken sliding. He deliberately touched the tip of his tongue along her teeth. Jane shuddered.

He removed his hands. Only lips touching lips. All movement stopped. The kiss poised on edge, timeless, eyes closed yet seeing all. Like flux melting silver, the kiss opened a soulful tunnel linking them. She could feel all the way down to him. They kissed with only the subtlest movements, tiny quivers along the walls of the ethereal tunnel – each open, heart to heart.

Thrilling, such surprise and delight, not to move, to

even utter a sound of joy. Never to disturb something so
precious.

Jane lifted her mouth away. The long chamber of the
kiss parted, delicately, peacefully.

"Oh Hovey."

"You wanted to be kissed."

"I didn't know. What was that?"

"Touching somewhere."

He lifted her in his arms and carried her limp body
three steps to the bed and stood her next to it. She smiled
small, like a wood nymph dazed from sleep and wine –
and an eternal kiss. Hovey waited. She eased the camisole
off her shoulders and helped it slip down, letting it pool
in a heap around her toes. The naked nymph eased onto
the bed, settling face up with legs closed. Her arms fell
like a halo around her head.

Hovey slipped into the bed, not touching her
anywhere. He waited until her eyes opened. Then his
right hand fit over her right thigh.

"Oh."

"Do you want?"

She nodded.

"Show your willingness, Jane."

She parted thighs. As last night, his hand fit the vee to
cover.

"My hand belongs here."

"Yes. Touch me."

The West is wild, rugged, and might be thought cruel.
The place for implacable unsentimental realists, men of
stern action. Hovey's touch must be impossible then,
because he is of The West, yet his tender caressing of her
sex became so sensitive and generous her heart struggled
to believe. She had asked for this act with intention – to

break her fear, in a bleak corner of her soul, that no such man exists.

She could not speak.

His mouth lowered to hers.

She tilted to accept.

The enchanted tunnel returned. They touched ... somewhere.

His fingers parted the lips below. He stirred the liquids. The bud accepted his touch directly, eager for attention. Two fingers eased apart the inner flesh and slipped inside, deep. Jane nearly wept with the blossoming of both sunbursts, the one above, the other below, knowing no difference.

His mouth, his fingers, his being, held the embrace whole. She surrendered entirely, floating, expanding, groaning as if wounded by delicious poison, until her limbs shuddered wild, until the flood a woman does not fear drowned her, if only for a moment.

~~~~~

In the night, Hovey woke, in need. He had accidentally fallen asleep in a woman's bed. Twelve hours since erupting in the livery stable, after so much kissing, after so much skin to skin with a young woman whose squeals of keen pleasure under his hand still echoed in his ears ... he needed. Jane lay on her stomach, breathing deeply.

His hand on her lower back caused only a faint stir. He moved it up between shoulder blades. A sigh. He pressed his body along her side, deliberately including the erect and impatient phallus. Jane stretched, elongating, but did not turn over. He moved the hand to her bottom, holding it as he might her breast. The flesh, firm. Supple. Shifting from one mound to the other brought only another sigh of her sleepy voice. Then … her right leg curled and lifted along the sheet. Hovey came above and behind, took organ in hand, and guided it home.

In the quiet and dark, with the potbelly's fire nearly out, he loosed his desire, thrusting smoothly from behind, with a grunt on each echoing around the room. Never one to require hundreds, now his path shortened – because a firm squeeze of soaking flesh greeted each penetration. With a cry, he forced the final one deep and held it embedded for emptying, emptying.

Hovey collapsed next to Jane, pulling a blanket over them both. She never spoke or stirred. He fell asleep.

~~~~~

6:22 a.m.

Will Hovey finished dressing. Jane stood at his side, nakcd and proud.

"This room is yours …"

"Until I don't want it anymore," she said. "It's not for guests."

"Does anyone ever come in here?"

"Never. I'm not a guest. I work for it."

"Have you been kissed now, Jane Cady Whitfield?"

Her eyes sparkled. Then they sobered.

"How did you know how?"

"In Laredo, Marguerite told me how to be gentle, to be slow. To kiss like that. She said, 'Breathe her breath. Drink the syrup she offers on her tongue. You will turn her into fire'."

Jane's eyes grew enormous. She took a step back.

"Yes."

He faced her dangerously.

"Yesterday in the livery?"

"Yes?"

"Something Marguerite told me. To take like that."

Jane nodded, transfixed.

"Like a wild buck running down a doe."

She nodded again.

"You will not lock the door. I will enter day or night to take you."

She sucked in a big breath.

"Say otherwise now," he said, "or it will be like that."

She did not speak.

He tore his eyes from hers and walked out.

part 3
july-august 1895

the ecstatic anguish of wonder

j.j.kirnan

July 29th, 1895
Monday
Silver City, New Mexico

When Jane opened the door to her room after work
the next day, expecting he would still be occupied in the
livery, her error caused shock. He grabbed her around the
waist and carried her to the bed. She threw up a barrage of
"no" but that was not the word they had agreed would
pause things. Hovey took her from behind again, but this
time against thrashing, swearing, and fingernails
deployed. He finished fast. She pulled away and huddled
in the corner of the bed against the wall, glaring at his
heaving body. Jane got even, outlasting him by patience
and silent imploring for fair treatment. She made him
kiss. She made him enter her sex from behind, sliding
cock with deep sure rhythm, his fingers on her vibrating
gland, thrusting steadily and caressing until she exploded,
twice. They woke in the night for more.

July 30th, 1895
Tuesday
Silver City, New Mexico

He disappeared for the evening. For hours it made her
nervous with expectation. At midnight she heard gravel
thrown at her window. Cautiously cracking open the
door, she found a note on the ground. It ordered her to
come to his room. She knew where it was, yet had not
entered it. She arrived with a robe over a nightdress and
knocked quietly. Ready for anything. The room was dark

and mysterious. He drew her inside, cautioned quiet, and kissed her. She wanted to not trust the gentleness, to stay on guard against a burst of taking, but his mouth melted her, and she yielded. Hovey tied her wrists with a cotton belt and fixed them above her head to a bar above the door. Gradually, his kisses on her neck and below caused the robe to part. He opened the buttons of the nightdress and kissed her breasts for so long Jane thought the sun would rise. Tied, she could not prevent the infuriating lovely kisses. Eventually, he spun her against the door and penetrated her flesh. Hovey finished first again but continued thrusting, cradling her breasts from behind as Jane achieved with exquisite pleasure, holding back screams, hanging from a pinnacle far on high.

July 31st, 1895
Wednesday
Silver City, New Mexico

7:45 p.m.
They worked so hard at jobs earlier, ardor went quiet in the evening. She had the day off tomorrow – he was not wanted until noon. They lay naked on the bed. Not aroused.

"Maybe it's my flow. It will start day after tomorrow, Hovey. Once mother told me things got quiet right before."

"You mother talked to you about that?"

"Yes. She made me learn my ... cycle, she called it. I was to always know. For safety, she said. And she talked about sex, some. Father did not realize all that."

A wave of sorrow swept over. She hated and loved

that it would never end, for all her life, pain from the death of her loved ones.

"It is remarkable how open you talk about this. Most women do not. Or they talk crude."

"Mother made me unshameful about it."

"It is good."

"It's remarkable you don't start something anyway, right in this bed, right this minute."

"You do not want?"

"No."

They breathed together in the bed. Remarkable how comfortable.

"Do you feel the urge now? Even a little."

Jane stayed silent, searching for the embers of her libido.

"Yes. Some."

"You can make it grow. It is your heat, it is good. A man can be brought to hardness easily. Make him hard. Then he will take you. Get him excited, you will be excited."

"Yes."

"Or ... you take over the bed."

"What?"

"Do what I tell you now, Jane."

Her breathing accelerated, lying beside him on his right.

"Touch me."

Her hand found the phallus. It was half-hard. The exotic way of it – soft skin sliding against firm shaft, its shape compelling it with unmistakable intent to penetrate something.

"Yes, yes," he said. He shifted to give her a better angle. Quickly Jane pulled it into a strong erection, pulsing and eager.

"Swing on top."

She gave a giggle and rolled onto his body, thighs apart, knees on either side of his torso. Her hand held the vibrant thing.

"Look right in my eyes, and put it in."

"Don't you want to take me from behind like a wild buck?"

"No. Sink down, fill yourself with it."

She almost failed to look in his eyes as ordered. He grunted to object. Then Jane's pride rose – she offered her visage to him, naked as her slender body. Hovey held her gaze. She slithered down and let the shaft part the lips, ease in, and push her insides apart, making her weight tell until fully impaled.

"Oh oh oh," she sighed. Her eyes closed. Breathless to have a cock thrust up in her body once again.

"Not to give me pleasure, Jane. Move to give it to yourself. Find the way."

"Oh no."

"Find your pleasure."

Jane shifted her hips. An immortal dance began. Rocking. Squeezing. Sliding.

She changed position, getting off her knees, with feet flat on the bed in a deep crouch. This added power. She leaned forward, setting hands on his chest. Now the shaft pulled and rubbed as well as impaled. Her breasts dropped down to him and inevitably his hands contained them.

"Mmm. Hmmm. Oh."

"Yes."

"Fuck," she grunted.

"Yes."

Her movements accelerated. Lubrication accelerated. The salacious sound of sex filled the bed. Her fingernails dug into his chest, short of breaking the skin – he did not object.

"Virgin to vixen in four days," he said.

"Yes!"

Now everything accelerated. The rightness of 'this way' took hold – apparently women had soared and slid on top during the past million years, and Jane inherited the knack.

"Whoa, wrow, oh, oh, oh, uh uh uh uh!"

In bed with Hovey, Jane had become eager. Virgin eager, woman eager ... shameless to find the joy ... quickly with a flush of red on her chest and cheeks, breath in gulping bursts, wide eyes announcing the sudden appearance of a luscious destination.

Jane rode home.

"Yaa, yaa, oh, oh, yes, yes, yes." Then ... "Ohhh!" With a brilliant contraction, she collapsed forward onto Hovey, shuddering, laughing, delirious.

"You want."

Jane gave a blubbering laugh. She quaked, breathing in heaves. She squeezed repeatedly around the gloriously stiff thing embedded in her sex.

Hovey let her vibrate and hum until she finally could speak.

"Girl on top. That's not against the law?"

"I will tell the sheriff you asked."

Her quakes slowly subsided, with involuntary jerks causing a tiny "oh" from her lips. Her breathing calmed.

"Hovey, you are still hard."

"Yes."

"In a few –"

"Stop! You do not care."

She laughed. She did not care about any man's needs, really – at this moment. She kept squeezing her muscles around cock to wring out every drop of pleasure nature offered.

"Fuck," she said.

"You can use me like this anytime, Jane Whitfield. Go again."

"Not yet."

"Go quick."

"Not yet."

"Then stay still. I like having your body on mine."

"I'm all wet."

He reached down and took the mounds of her bottom in his hands, pulled them hard to force his organ deep. She tightened around. It shot off a strong contraction rippling through her pelvis.

"Oh no oh no oh no Hovey oh no I like fucking so much on top or bottom just fuck me and fuck me and finish me down to the last drop and the world can go to hell."

"After last night, you know you can finish more than once."

"Yes yes yes yes yes."

"It is good with fingers and cock at the same time."

"Yes yes yes yes yes."

"There is something I left out the other night, about the girls down the street."

"Huh?"

"Miss Honeyhurst's girls."

"What?"

"I said they never finish. That is true, when servicing a gentleman caller."

"So?"

"They do finish, Jane. Alone in their beds."

She went silent, her head on his chest, the hard cock still pushed up inside. He tipped them over onto their sides, face to face, and withdrew from her body.

"What are you doing?"

He put his hand between her thighs. Jane shuddered.

"You could go up again, right now, by hand."

"Do it."

"No."

Jane pretended she did not understand. He did not pretend she did not understand.

"Touch," he said, and took his hand away.

"Hovey ..."

"Touch."

Her modesty shook. She rotated onto her other side, facing away from him. She lay perfectly still.

"I can't."

"Because I am watching?"

"Yes. No."

Hovey remained silent.

"It's selfish," she said.

He waited.

"I can't."

"Did someone tell you it is a sin?"

"Yes."

"They think sex is only holy for making children."

"Oh."

"And you cannot make a baby by touching yourself."

She laughed. Who knew William Hovey was a philosopher?

"Jane, we have greatly sinned for four days."

"Yes, we will go to hell for sure."

"Do you feel shame?"

"No."

"That is the biggest sin of all."

She laughed hard and spun onto her back.

"It was not my father or mother. But they didn't tell me sex was holy just for pleasure, either. Not right out. There were plenty of people in Ithaca calling it a sin."

"Your pleasure in sex is beautiful."

"Are you going to tell the sheriff that too?"

"Yes."

"I do want to fly up again. Please touch me."

"I did not do anything just now, with you on top. You flew up on your own. So fast. I was only the stiff rod."

Jane froze in place.

His serious intense voice said, "I want ... to watch ... while you do it ... with your fingers."

"Hovey ..."

"You are already halfway there, after that big finish just now. Can you feel that?"

"Yes. It's beating like a heartbeat."

"Touch."

She steadied her breath. She closed her eyes. Her hand found the way, as her ancestor-sisters had for hundreds of millennia. Hovey inched aside, not the best angle for observing the caresses, but perfect to watch the expression on her face.

Jane, nineteen, delighted to take instruction from Will Hovey, twenty-four – when she wanted to. Her sexual soul had expanded with grand joy over the four days of sin. However, no woman needs instruction or training for self-pleasure – only the shameless self-sanction to do it. Hovey said not a word.

Two fingers of her right hand separated the lips, with reluctance for them to part, due to dew on the delightful petals. A finger eased up and down between. Her thumb needed no instruction – it took control of the bud nestled in folds. This wonderful thing was sticky with her liquids and swollen from agitation during her ride on top rubbing rubbing rubbing against stiff cock.

Gradually, Jane's thighs parted. She arched up from the bed a fraction with each brush of fingers. The familiar assent began. She greeted it with an uninhibited moan. Her left hand joined. She made it the queen of the clitoris. The queen could not yet touch her subject directly, did well to press the skin of the hood, urging the bud to arousal. The fingers of Jane's right hand went deep. They seemed inclined to caress the inside-underside of vagina.

"Yes," she whispered. "Yes. Yes."

The strangeness, to have someone watching … the disapproval, pleasure for pleasure's sake … these doubts hovered behind her closed eyes and pooled in her chest. Then, her fingers took her past reluctance. With bravery they opened the good world beyond. Her body warmed with the clean exuberance to be alive, stroked to gentle fire by her will.

She caressed faster. Her need became urgent. Strong. Noisy. The thrashing hands drew liquids down. The gland vibrated, all the flesh swelled, all the muscles contracted in one final clench. And … release.

"Awoh, oohho, oh oh oh." Jane's eyes opened in amazement. "Oh no oh oh Oh!"

Her thighs shuddered violently. A spray of liquid shot forth. Words burbled through racing breath. The queen of the clitoris had won. Her hands fell away, hips sunk into the bed, and tears flowed. She turned on her side and fell silent.

If there is a god, or Venus, she must bless this sacrament. Didn't she send a witness?

Hovey lay next to the limp body of Jane Whitfield, its tearful face pointed away. Eventually, it spoke.

"Hovey."

"Yes?"

"That was heaven."

"Yes. I saw you go there. You were singing and laughing."

"Will you let me touch any time I want?"

"You do not need me to say."

"I can't believe it's free, so ..."

"Jane."

"All my life I never touched it, never exploded. No one told me I could. Please tell me I can."

"Jane."

"Okay. I give myself permission."

Hovey waited. She sighed with finality, and turned over to face him – languorous melted female.

"Bliss."

"Yes!"

"Now I need your cock again."

"You are trying to prove ten times. Women ten times men."

"Yes. I need eight more." She propped up on one elbow. A moist, blustery face with a grin.

"Did you like watching?"

"Yes. You lost your shyness of it."

"I guess so. Will Hovey, watching his woman wiggle and sing."

"Yes."

"I'm all ripe here. Come get it."

"Do it to yourself again. I like watching. Do it again."

"No. You. Do you have the appetite? The hunger to?"

"Watching stirred it up. See?"

"Please fill me with that. I want to feel the splash."

At his first movement, Jane's legs opened like wings. She lay back, with right arm outstretched overhead. Her left hand caressed, between. Two whispers of delight escaped.

Hovey positioned above. With organ in hand, he made the connection, smooth, slippery, with mutual small cries of happiness from each. Jane's now-educated fingers circled the embedded shaft and resumed her new favorite thing to do on earth, teasing the pearl in the vee.

"Close your legs," he said, raising his so hers could slide together under. Then he lifted her left hand away, moving the arm up above her head on the bed to cross wrists with the other. With his weight supported on left forearm and lower legs, his right arm circled her torso and drew her waist in an arc off the bed.

Jane was taken up into his arms. Her breasts touched his chest. The intimacy, the vicinity of mouths, the easy glances into each other's eyes – she heated everywhere.

Then, he eased forward, up her body, pressing her hips with his. The shaft pushed deeper, and with perfect angle the base of it slid against the roof of vagina. Their mons rubbed, with the pearl between.

"Oh," she whispered.

"Yes."

Hovey began rocking. With his weight not resting on her, she could rock back. They kissed sex to sex. It was exciting right away.

"This is beautiful."

"Yes."

Then they kissed mouth to mouth. Gentle at first, then seeking, probing, soaking. Jane's hands remained crossed above her head, impatient, but obedient to her self-binding. To fight frustration, she swayed her torso against his and increased the strength of rubbing below.

"Oh, oh."

His rhythm came in slow waves, sometimes thrusting, sometimes subtly swaying to squash against her organs. Hovey pulled her in with his encircling right arm. The way it wrapped her – how her slenderness must please – the graceful bending of her torso when he clasped her close. Supple flexing, bent like a bow of yew wood pulled taut by a man. Jane loved her body in this instant.

"I wish my arms free."

"Do it."

She wrapped her arms around his neck. Now their tryst became a full embrace. Her mouth came to his ear.

"Caught up in your arms, Hovey. Naked in thy embrace. Love me with your body. Kiss me, kiss me."

He invaded her mouth, stroking her tongue with wet lips, while liquids flowing below lubricated the joining.

The bed caught fire. The rocking motion sent his hard flesh into her soft. She squirmed under it, rocking back at him. They reached a profound dance, old as loving, but new to their young union. It was in the kiss no less than the dance of hips. She tangled her fingers in his hair and urged his head forward, pulling his lips and tongue deep into her mouth. The power in his thrusts jolted her pelvis, crushing the entirety of the liquid yoni.

She tore out of the kiss and threw her head back. "Oh, fuck me to the end!"

Jane's chest filled with holy greed. To ascend. To ride each rocking thrust with eyes wide, staring into the void.

"Yes. Yes. Yes!" Then her voice froze, her pelvis coiled – while the relentless man-organ penetrated her center four, five, six times.

To explode like a bursting star.

To scream like a queen shattering the night.

"Yi yi aoh ohhh oh oh."

She screamed again. No words might be heard in it – only the ecstatic anguish of wonder.

Ignoring her thrashing body, groans torn from her throat, heedless of juice gushing, Hovey penetrated with surety – to reach something yet untouched – the profound virginity.

Jane sought to avoid. To end. To float. He was too certain they should not. She fell apart completely, her hands untwining from around his neck to fall to the bed. The phallus went home as never before.

"Oh, oh, oh. Oh no. Oh no."

Then his ending thrusts. She knew them now. He took her along. No muscles with which to clench and release – all melted. Instead, the new explosion filled her body from belly to fingertips, her soul to bursting.

Hovey's thrusts slowed, now massive, long, intentional. On the last heroic penetration, he emptied into her utterly, moaning like a beast rampaging in the wild.

He collapsed, pressing her into the bed, rolled aside. Jane quivered next to him, half intertwined, entirely finished to the last spent end. She began to weep. With no strength left on earth, she could not protect her emotion. A teardrop in her hurt heart broke loose, and the liquid of it flowed from her throat.

"The last thing my brother said ... 'I wanted to be a man'."

They fell asleep.

2:27 a.m.

They awoke, hungry.

"It's not all sex," she said.

They dressed partially, Jane in a long night shirt that draped to the thigh. Hovey, breeches and suspenders. Jane liked his chest bare, luxurious with brown hair and a glimmer of auburn.

Apples, cheese, bread and butter, cider, chocolate. Jane had secured this meal earlier, hidden in a special box with drainage for melting ice that kept things cool. They sat at a small table in her room.

"This is the food I cannot get on the trail."

"What do you eat?"

"I only eat meat on the trail."

He chose bread over the other selections. And chocolate.

"Tell me again why you don't mind I am not pretty."

"What did I say that first night?"

"That I have the most beautiful body of any woman you ever saw."

"Ever had. Yes."

"Now that you have thoroughly ravished it, is it still?" She said the word with girlish sarcasm. It had become a permanent silly thing to say instead of the other word. They liked it.

"You have no reluctance to speak of this?"

"None."

"Yes. The more I ravish, the more beautiful."

"Ravish me, Hovey."

They stood up and cleared away their meal. Jane would wash up later. When both came to a full stop, standing six feet apart, she resumed.

"You don't mind I am not pretty?"

"You are angry."

"Yes, but you don't mind I'm not beautiful?"

"The anger is beautiful."

Jane went silent.

"There is no hate in it," he said, with certainty.

She turned to look away.

"Hovey ..."

"Your feet are beautiful."

She burst out laughing. Now she could look in his face. Her hand came to it, caressing gently. She touched his high cheekbones again.

"Where did these come from?"

"Tsézhiné."

"What?"

"I have four parents of parents. Mother of mother was Tsézhiné, pure. She had them."

"What about the other three?"

"One Mestizo, two white."

"So, I ended my virginity with a mongrel dog." He smiled, because Jane sent delight with her joke. "What is Tsézhiné?"

"Apache. It means 'Black Rock'."

"You are beautiful," she whispered.

Hovey took the hem of the night shirt and lifted it over her head. A wave of shy washed past, but did not linger. She crossed the room and twirled. She posed. She turned here and there, to show her breasts. Hovey sat on the edge of the bed to watch. Talking would stir him up. She was not done.

"Where did you learn that last thing, Hovey. You know, to hintch up on me and rub like that?"

"Well ..."

"Wait. Marguerite, right?"

"No. Someone else."

"It is good for the girl. I went all the way up twice."

"Yes. The girl likes being rubbed like that."

"That was deep, how deep you went in me. While still rubbing. It made me come up so fast."

He sat silent. She drifted around, always turning to present her nude body in provocation, aware of his fascination with her breasts. She crossed her hands over her chest – not hiding the tips, however.

"I know you like them."

"Yes."

"The nips get big when you look at them like this. Or when your mouth is on them."

She bent from the waist to fetch a wisp of cotton floating on the floor. The soft flesh dropped like hanging fruit on a bending branch. Coming upright, she placed her forearms on top of her head. The lifting made the tips tip up.

"I wish I could tell them to fill with milk, to tempt you to drink."

"Yes."

"Or whiskey!"

Jane saw it make the organ twitch against his trousers. She was hungry for it. She ordered him to drop the britches. He lay down prone on the bed. Highly aroused.

"Fetch a cloth," he said.

She gave a squeal and scrambled to do it, walking fast to the bedside with a towel dampened from a kettle near the fire. She reached toward the intended organ.

"No."

She froze.

Hovey took the towel from her hand.

"How eager you are to have it in your mouth."

"Yes, Hovey. I like doing it."

"So do I."

Jane's eyes widened. She stopped breathing. Hovey offered no relief from the truth. The intention. The inevitable. He took her by the waist and tumbled her body into the bed on her back.

"No."

"Yes."

A modesty remaining from her beautiful virginity rose up. Jane's eyes squinted shut. Her thighs pressed together.

"No."

"Yes."

He propped up on his left elbow, right hand sliding inside her thigh. She did not yield.

"You must have thought about it."

Jane shook her head no, lying.

"It is the next thing. Let me."

Chest heaving, she squeezed legs together. Then, she could not deny the exciting thought of it. Her legs parted. Hovey cleaned the inside of her thighs and all else between. Then he fit his hand snug in the vee and cupped fingers around the soft apricot. Wishing to be constrained yet again, though he did not require, she lifted hands up, wrists crossed above her head on the bed. She needed slow time and deep breaths to bear the exposure.

"I only cleansed you to start new. Do not hold back, Jane. You drank my juice with pleasure."

She nodded, not lying.

"You drank it."

"Yes."

"Now I will drink yours. Do not hold it back."

Hovey moved between. She closed her eyes. Something with soft bristle of beard brushed her thigh. A warm breath flowed there. A parting of his lips opened hers.

So sensitive his kiss.

So inquisitive, his tongue.

So sure, his confidence.

The fresh juice flowed.

She wished to be bound no longer. Her hands came below. One fit her thigh and pulled it wide. The other fit behind his head, and with a subtle guiding he might only know as a dream, she urged him on, asked him in, gave her quickening sex like a holy offering.

Jane's last sane thought rushed by, chased by a goddess' pleasure run amok – a man does not need to give this act, since it is his world. Hovey must want it. Want her. He must truly desire the melding of his mouth and her trembling, drenched yoni. The thought blinded her with passion. She wished she could drink with him this very moment.

Then the world of thought vanished. His tongue reached in and slipped across the roof of her vagina, where the underside of woman's organ of pleasure waited. The unseen goddess unleashed the silver rain. Jane screamed to the helping angels, who sent their love.

3:40 a.m

Hovey woke. He had forgotten to feel trapped by falling asleep in a woman's bed. Jane was fussing and mumbling, with eyes shut tight. At the call of her name, they opened, filled with tears.

"You are crying in your sleep."

She blinked to the surface, yet stayed at the edge of the

night-world. With one final quake and a sobbing sigh, she settled.

"Finishing," she said, eking it out from her sleepy self. "I dreamed finishing just now. Many times. Hovey, can you believe it? I dreamed finishing sex. There was wet everywhere. I could almost taste it."

"Oh."

"It was so real. How thrilling it is, bursting into glory."

"Yes."

"With your mouth on me ... that was ... magnificent."

"Oh."

"I was not of this earth. Not of."

"Saying that kind of thing will make me do it again. Many times."

"Put your mouth on me every night."

"I will."

"Is it ... disgusting?"

Hovey did not answer immediately. She suddenly feared to hear him say 'yes.' She held her breath.

"Your shyness for it ... was fine to see. Fine you have something that does not belong to me. Do not give up that modesty too easily. The rough cowboy tries to get it. Keep it. Give it, but keep it."

"Oh."

"Because the modesty could melt away forever, with what I am about to say."

"I will keep."

"Always be a little shy when you see I want to do it."

"I will."

Hovey paused for one instant. It made room for his next move.

"It is not disgusting. The opposite. It is delicious. I

crave it madly."

"Oh!"

"It is pleasure ... to take the scent and taste. To drink it."

"Hovey ..."

"I want it. I could drink it for hours. On the trail, I miss it desperate."

She quivered with the thrill of a man saying this to her. She was specifically aware of the tender lips and the orifice between them. Her pelvis contracted.

"I want it. Greedy. But never give it if you are too shy, or just to please me."

"Oh. Oh."

"Did you like your ending from it?"

"It was in my dream."

"Dream it often, Jane. I will make it come true."

"You will put your mouth on me?"

"Yes."

Ragged from emotion, still partly asleep, she lay with a warm glow of beauty and peace between her thighs.

"I hope I dream of all these finishings every night. So sweet, dreams."

"I dream of it sometimes."

"Mother gave me a novel once, there was a poem in it that I read over and over. I didn't believe the poem. Didn't believe it was about a real thing. I thought it was the imaginary wish of a romantic girl. Now I know better."

"What poem?"

Jane sighed. She came a little more awake. She remembered.

"There were words that broke in utterance,

melted in the fire.
Embrace, that was convulsion ...
Then a kiss as long and silent as the ecstatic night,
and deep, deep, shuddering breaths,
which meant beyond whatever could be
told by word or kiss."

{From the novel "Aurora Leigh" by
Elizabeth Barrett Browning, 1856}

They were so exhausted they began to drift back to
sleep, with the reverberant poem hovering. Then her
voice called him back.
"Please, Hovey."
He stirred.
"I want to give the fresh juice again."

4:02 a.m.
Hovey began dressing, with a glance at the door – and
a glance at Jane – naked, half under the covers.
"Hovey. Get back in this bed. We are going to end the
night sleeping together. Walk through town at dawn to
have breakfast at that cantina on Santa Rita Street. They
open early, for workers."
"You could lose your job, Jane, if the hotel only likes
chaste single girls working for them."
"They look the other way. Two others I know are not
married and working in the kitchen and ... being unchaste
at night."
"Not if you are seen with me in public. Many people
in Silver City think I am shiftless, strange, a killer of wild
beasts, a heathen, a seducer of women. Devilish. Evil.
That is why I stay here, south side. I come and go easy

from here."

"I don't care. Get back in this bed."

"A man wants to get away fast after ravishing."

"Yes."

"A free man does not fall asleep with the woman."

"I know."

"I should disobey you, just to show I am a man." He began taking off his clothes.

"If you are not a man right now, my hand will fix that as soon as you get in this bed. Now come here."

He walked to her. She held open the blankets.

"Besides," she said, "I am still curious about ten. Ten times. You didn't take me there yet."

"Really."

"Yes. Now get in here and give me another one."

"To be ordered around by a nineteen-year-old girl ..."

"Girl? If I'm not a woman right now, your fucking cock will fix that."

"Girl with a vile mouth. Not much of a virgin."

Shortly, the fucking cock penetrated the vile girl all the way to her cervix.

"Not much of," she said, groaning and laughing.

9:12 a.m.

They slept through their breakfast plan. They decided to not be seen together in public. Yet.

"Are you allowed to have meals in the hotel dining room?"

"Yes," she said. "We get half-off the price."

"Here are my instructions ..."

Jane's hand came to her mouth in mirth. "Are we going to have sex in the dining room?"

"No. I am going to my room now. You might have

the day off, but I have to start work in two hours. I will get food on my own. Get dressed now, then come to my room. I will give you money for your meal. And more instructions."

He did not wait to see if she objected. He turned and left.

"I have my own money," she said to the back of the door.

Half an hour later, in the broad morning, Jane stole to Hovey's room wearing a flower-print dress, the only one that survived the flood. An element of danger filled her. She half-believed no one knew about ... "them." Especially Sam Thomson, the owner of the livery stable. She was reckless, however – *so what if he catches me?*

Hovey let her in. His hair and bare chest were wet, and he wore only snug britches that cinched in his waist. They were wet. Jane was hungry, but seeing him this way made her *hungry*.

"Have whatever you want." He handed her several small coins. "Return here."

"I have my own money." She handed the coins back. Hovey nodded.

She waited for more orders. His face remained stern. Then, his hands dipped under the hem of the dress and slid up her body to the waistband of her undergarment. Jane sucked in a breath. Looking in her eyes, he pulled the thing down to the floor around her ankles. He moved back. Jane stepped out of the knickers and kicked them aside. She was breathing fast, showing defiance in her face.

"Sit alone at a table. Let yourself look like a woman seeking to be taken."

She nodded.

"Others will try to sit with you. Men. You will say, 'thank you, but I am dining only with myself this morning'."

She nodded.

"Think about what will happen to you when you return to this room."

Jane's grit stirred. She said not a word. She opened the door and stepped outside into the late morning brilliance.

~~~~~

An hour later, Jane raced up to his door. She swung it open and barged in. If he snatched her up for rough penetration, she would surrender totally or fight like hell – she was so aroused by her erotic nothing-under meal she wanted sex either way. Immediately.

Hovey stood at a table across from the door. His dress had not changed. She charged at him.

"Stop."

She stopped. In amazement.

"Something happened," he said.

"What?"

"Telegram. Delivered right after you left."

"What is it?"

He did not turn his visage away. "I am leaving Silver City in an hour, Jane."

Like a slap across the face, yet her head did not jolt aside.

"It is from –"

She screamed. "Don't tell me." Her flaming eyes held his.

"Okay."

She looked away, gazing at fate. One fist balled into a

knot. Hovey went silent while she heaved three big breaths.

"Is everything you own, except your horse, in this room?"

"Yes."

"When you ride away, will it all be gone?"

"Yes."

She turned her fiery eyes on him now, letting a long beat of time pass.

"You will do what I say, Will Hovey." He nodded. She led him to the door. "I will have you one more time." He nodded again. "Put your hands against the door."

Jane bound him with imaginary ties, fixing his hands at his side, flat against the wood door. She crouched down and unbuckled his breeches. The beautiful phallus of this man leapt into her hand, this man who had opened her, taken her, and on times submitted to her.

Her hand brought the erection fully tumescent. She stood and lifted the hem of her dress, pressed him close, fit her sex to his, and eased them together. She looked right into his eyes, all the way in. Her entire being coiled, ready to ravish.

Her rage had no hate in it.

Only pain.

Her eyes clouded over. She jerked off and away, her dress falling to cover. Without a glance into his eyes, she pushed him away from the door and ran out.

part 4
august 1895

all passion befitting

August 10, 1895
Saturday
West of Silver City, New Mexico

... ten days later.

By sundown of his eastward ride to Silver City, Will
Hovey reached his favorite spot on the Lithy, forty-five
miles from town. He had followed the stream downhill to
the southeast eight miles after meeting it. He made camp.
He examined the hoofs of his horse, checked him all
around, and set a bag with oats on a strap around his neck
while he brushed him down. He tethered him long within
reach of good grass at the edge of the river.

All day in the saddle brought stiffness. He welcomed
the movement required to gather wood and set up his
little lean-to canvas shelter. All the while, he could not
shake the feeling that had taunted him all day, pressure on
his chest from riding directly toward the woman. They
had parted rudely ten days back. He had barely thought
of her all the past week. Now the burn of her loomed up,
strong enough to trigger an urge to spin around and
escape the heat.

However, he could not avoid Silver City. His mission
required at least two days there, with details and
preparation for the journey back to the Gila River, from
whence he departed early this morning.

He waded in the stream. Swift now in early August
following the July New Mexico monsoons, the Lithy
would dwindle soon, but not falter completely. He liked
knowing the stream would be on his left for a while
tomorrow. The music of it would soothe. Perhaps.

He decided to turn in early, after a quick meal of

bacon and bread, not even making coffee. He needed sleep. With a decision to ride again before dawn to reach Silver City by noon, he slipped into his trail bed.

August 11, 1895
Sunday
Six miles east of Silver City, NM

10:00 a.m.

With the sun ascending, Hovey reached a bend in the trail only six miles from town, having left the Lithy behind. Then, something odd. A signpost. As he approached, it was unreadable. Whatever it said must be on the town-facing side. This trail was little-used – a sign was an odd joke. He rode to it, and around. It appeared brand new.

It said, "Jane."

With an arrow pointing to the left, south.

This could not be. No. No.

Bolting off the trail, he found tracks, urged his horse into a gallop, and raced down a slope onto flat ground around a spur. A mile on he saw the windmill. The reservoir. The ranch house.

Then, a Jane. On the porch of the house, with hand on brow looking back at his approach. Within ten seconds, he knew for certain. His Jane.

He wove through the double fencing via gaps, jerked to a halt at the porch and launched off the horse. Jane's hand covered her mouth, her eyes huge. They started shouting at the same time.

"What the hell are you doing here?"

"No no no you are not here no no no."

"What is this place?"

"William Hovey get off my land."

"What?"

"Get on that damn horse and get damn off my land."

He strode right up, climbing two steps to the porch.

"What?"

"This is my ranch, now get out of here."

"You cannot put up a sign like that."

"Get out."

"That will attract rats."

"Rats?"

"Every rat bastard in these mountains."

"You can't be here, you can't."

"What do you mean this is yours?"

"This is my land my ranch my windmill."

"What?"

"That sign is for the windmill man."

Hovey took a step back. This was impossible.

"Who?"

"The windmill man. He's due here any minute I had to put the sign, he'd never find this place. He's coming to see if the windmill could work."

"How is this your place?"

"You never asked where I went that day of the storm. You just pulled me off my horse, slammed me against the wall, tied me up, and fucked me."

Hovey nearly slapped her face. His hand stopped. What she said was true.

"Then you abandoned me so fast it never came up."

Jane saw the look in his eye. Lust. She might have it in hers.

"Don't you dare touch me," she spat at him.

Hovey walked to the edge of the porch and surveyed

the property. This could have been a working homestead once. He peered at the windmill and reservoir. Jane saw it.

"This place is only good if I can get water out of the ground."

"Jane, do you at least have a rifle?"

"No."

Hovey shook his head in disgust.

Jane told how her uncle and aunt had abruptly departed the day after the flood destroyed their business two and half weeks ago, how they willed this property to her. Hovey walked inside the ranch house. Jane did not follow. When he emerged, they stood six feet apart with a slight wind blowing, swirling the dust the place was made of.

"What are you doing here?"

Hovey told. How an opportunity he had been seeking suddenly came to fruition and required fast action and decision. It consisted of a permit to run three hundred head of cattle on the Gila River on a prescribed range, including the option of purchasing two-year-old cows for $22 per head. He already had the funding. It came from Marguerite and her partner in Laredo, who trusted him. They would supply $4000, and Hovey the remainder.

"You have twenty-six hundred dollars?"

"Yes. Saved from an inheritance and government contracts to supply game. Took me six years to save. The army pays well."

"I thought you were a scraggly poor hunter, homeless and wandering."

"No."

The staggering amounts of money brought Jane up short. She looked around. How much money would it take to make this ranch go?

"In a year, the herd will sell for $60 per head. We hope."

"But why are you here if the cows are there?"

"All the details have to be executed in Silver City. A bank in town knows me, will control the cash for me. There is a young man I know there I have a mind to hire. I had to head down to the Gila to make sure everything was set up first. I had to act fast."

Just then a lone rider came around the spur and rode toward the ranch. Before he arrived, Jane turned on Hovey.

"It hurt when you left like that. I didn't get a chance to release you to the wild."

Then they greeted the windmill man.

11:05 a.m.

It was going to take $55 to make the windmill operate. The water table was good. Jane learned how to bring up water with a hand pump the visitor got working, which required seventeen cycles before it flowed. Exhausting. Nevertheless, water waited beneath her feet.

The visitor was barely out of sight.

"You will be on the Gila River for a year?"

"Yes."

"How far?"

"A two-day easy ride. A person might make it early afternoon of the second day."

"You can't get your hands on my body from that far away, Hovey."

They flung themselves together, ecstatic in an enormous kiss. There was laughter in it, from the ridiculous coincidence and fate's joke on them. Then humor vanished – nothing is funny when blind with lust.

His mouth invaded hers, swimming in the wet. Her arms pulled them tight together.

They yanked the clothing from each other so urgently more than one button went flying. Then a beat of time four feet apart, staring in shock into each other's eyes. With a crazed screech, she leapt onto him, wrapping legs around his waist. He caught her well.

"Take me to the bedroom of my house," she cried, laughing at the world.

Hovey strode inside with Jane clinging to his torso, mouth like a viper's inflicted on his neck, stopping one room in, at a bed. They collapsed on it. In one powerful flow he pushed her legs high and wide, guided his organ, and plunged it into the flesh with a ripped thudding sound, like a fence post dropped on end in mud.

"Oh fuck fuck fuck," she screamed.

He slid out. "Up."

She fit hands behind knees and tugged, causing the mounded yoni to form up with utter exposure, gleaming with juice. He penetrated like a warrior.

"Oh oh oh no."

Hovey pulled out, gathered balance, and sunk deep with a shattering scream.

"Hrhhh yaah,"

The muscles of his back rippled and thighs shuddered as stark rhythm began.

"Fuck. Me. Please. Please. Fuck. Me. Fuck. Fuck. Fuck." She trailed off into delirium.

Hovey – fast and strong. He scooped huge gulps of air and grunted them out on each impaling. With no mercy in him, Jane bellowed frightened screams. They incited his furor, wrought each thrust gigantic in intention, ferocious and unstoppable.

He grabbed her around the waist, spun her onto her belly, forced her thighs apart and penetrated like a berserk god. His hips rotated hard against her bottom and the cock slammed deep.

Torso jammed into the bed, face buried in a pillow, Jane absorbed cruel pounding and the roar of a great beast in her ears. Never had such violence descended on her. Yet fear turned to greed. Her voice awoke.

"Please. Please. Hard. Harder. Please. Oh God, please. Hard."

Hovey's thrusting accelerated. His demented cries grew so fierce a new wave of fear flooded past her heart – yet she increased squeezing and shifted to help him find the deep. With every massive plunge, the shaft tugged at the bud atop her lips.

"Fuck me. Fuck. Me. There. There. Hard. Hard."

He stopped and flipped her onto her back. She pulled behind her thighs to expose fully, and he rammed home.

Jane first. A red flush appeared on her chest. Her face burned. She pulled back even more on her legs and arched her back off the bed. Her breath, her voice, her living organs seized – she could not prevent three, four, five gigantic thrusts penetrating her rigid body. The last one unfroze the she-beast roar.

"Haghaah...fuck! Oh ..."

– she shouted to the ceiling and collapsed to the bed, limbs quaking uncontrollably.

Hovey never relented. Thundering the louder, his last thrusts slammed into juice flooding the shuddering quim. With a final giant plunge, he spilled into the brimming lake of it.

11:30 a.m.

"What the hell was that?"

"We were holding back in town, not to make too much noise," he said.

"Yes. Out here I can scream to the mountaintops, and no one will come to pull you off my body."

"I can do whatever I want to you."

"Yes."

"Are you afraid?"

"Yes."

"Do you like it?"

"Yes."

They lay tangled on the bed.

"I have to get in town."

"It's Sunday, Hovey. No bank. Stay here until dawn tomorrow and make me afraid all night long."

"No. I am leaving in a few minutes."

"You'll get there, have nothing to do, and when your manly desires erupt again, you'll have to go to Miss Honeyhurst's, and that will make me wrathful and murderous, since you could have stayed here and made me scream all night. How many more do you have before dawn?"

"I was on the trail too long again. At least twice, probably more."

"More, since it is me."

"Since it is you."

That made Jane sigh. She could incite a man to many eruptions. Nineteen and ripe.

"Don't go."

Hovey rose from her arms and stood at the side of the bed, naked.

"Do you have any food?"

"Yes. I planned to stay all day and overnight 'til

tomorrow afternoon. Maybe Monday too. I have things in a cool-bag."

"What food?"

"Bacon, eggs, cheese, bread. A ham for dinner. Two jars of vegetables. The ice is about half melted, but the food is good."

"I have some food too."

"We have water now."

They were silent for a moment. Then Jane rose next to him. Likewise ... naked. She looked in his eyes.

"Did you have any woman since you ran out on me ten days ago?"

"No."

"What you just put on me, Hovey ... I felt ... like I was destroyed. Almost. What was that?"

"Possession. Rage to have you."

"Yes. Hovey, we don't have ordinary sex, do we?"

"No."

"That was taking, wasn't it? That was you taking me, fierce."

"Yes. Taking. Claiming."

"More than 'fucking'."

"Yes."

Jane paused for certainty.

"Every time you have rage to possess, take me hard like that, Hovey. Ravish me. I want it."

It sunk in like church reality. After a moment, he nodded, then spoke quietly.

"You know what to do if it becomes too fearful."

"I say 'stop'."

"Yes. Then what will happen?"

"You will stop."

He nodded. Serious.

Jane shook – this law made him much more dangerous.

"Are you hurt anywhere?"

She turned her body looking for bruises. Or blood. No blood, two bruises.

"You can also have me with tiny gentle kisses all night long."

"Yes."

"Tender and sweet sex."

"Yes."

Flushed with satisfaction, awed by the power of her body to ascend, aroused by the scent and sight of the man at her side – Jane turned a corner.

"I want you to never go to the bordello again. I want you to only have me. Only take me. I give myself completely."

Hovey did not look away from her eyes. He did not dim his. They held the tableau for ten seconds.

"I will be away for a year."

"Visit me here every month for two days."

"A long ride."

"We will time it to avoid my fertility."

"I cannot be away from the herd that long."

"Make your best cowhand a foreman five days out of each month."

"Risky."

"You'll probably have business to attend in Silver City every so often anyway."

"No. Wait ... maybe."

"You need the body of a woman to finish in, Hovey. Your hand can release you at night, but you need a woman's lips open for your kisses, her legs open, vagina open. Her screams in your ear. You need the taste and scent of her juices all over your mouth."

Hovey walked out onto the porch of the ranch house. She followed slowly, a warmth spreading in her center.

"Let it rest," he said. "I will stay the night here."

Jane laughed gaily.

"We're naked on the porch!" She came behind and asserted her body against his back, circling arms around his waist. "Just like every man, wanting to run for the hills after ravishing."

"Yes."

"But I'm too delicious for you."

"Yes, Jane Whitfield."

"You can have me ten times between now and tomorrow. No other man has ever been inside my body. I am your virgin that way. I treasure William Bennis Hovey is my only man ever."

She spun around to his front, wrapped her arms around his neck, pressed her breasts against his chest, and angled her head to take his kiss. It did not disappoint. Long, slow, sweet, and wet.

Then he lifted her and set her down facing out to the yard, at a railing that had survived the years of neglect. It was sturdy. From behind, he wrapped his right hand around her thigh and lifted the leg off the porch, setting the foot on the railing. She bent forward to accommodate, hands taking hold of the wood. Jane did not utter a sound.

Hovey crouched slightly, positioned perfectly, and from behind made the most gentle, sweet penetration ever dreamed. Like a chaste healing kiss on a beloved's forehead. He did not withdraw. They breathed together over it, one, two, three peaceful breaths.

Then, just as gently, he slid from her flesh, took three

steps to the right, and stood next to the railing, looking back at her body.

She lowered her leg. Lowered her gaze. Strolled to him. Eyes hidden. She knelt. Her hand circled the cock, wet from her wet. She moved carefully. The tip entered her mouth. She paused, relaxing, accepting, opening. Inclining forward, the cock inched in. Breathing around it, she held for the ripe moment. She leaned more. The phallus penetrated smoothly to the root, surrounded by her liquid mouth and throat.

"Oh ... oh," he sighed.

She drew off. She kept her eyes coyly turned away, yet let him see the corner of her glistening mouth with a little smile hiding. She stood and walked back to the other side of the porch. When he reached her, she still did not look in his eyes – a delightful tease, a token of modesty when they had become so carnal, one stroke at a time.

Yes, I am your half-shy half-virgin sweet
young girl. But I'll have your great rod
sliding down my throat, as deep as you want.

"You can be hard even though you finished already," she said, eyes downcast still.

"If it is you."

"If it is me."

"Hovey, can you save your next one until tonight?"

"Yes. But I will keep entering."

He lifted her foot up on the railing again, this time face to face. He lowered enough to fit, made cock fill vagina, pressing her body to stay buried for many seconds.

When he withdrew, she dropped her leg. He pulled her in with hands on the mounds of her bottom. Hard cock squashed against her belly. They did not separate – it became a warm sexual embrace, with small movements of flesh on flesh, Jane giving tiny exasperations of pleasure for the touching. Then she whispered, head resting on his chest.

"I don't believe it yet – having it in my body. A man enters me. Can that be? His sex, his cock, right up in my body. In vagina. I love to squeeze around it. Just that, cock in me. A cock fucking into me. A few days ago, I never knew. Now I crave it like thirst."

She slipped out of his arms and turned to the yard again, hands on the railing. She looked over her shoulder. Her eyes sought his.

"Please."

She bent her body into an s-shape and moved her feet apart. He positioned behind. With one hand around the shaft, he used the tip to caress and discover, to ease flesh aside until it found the willing opening. Jane was able to look back at him.

"Cock in me," she whispered.

The shaft slipped in. They steadied.

"I know you want to keep going."

"Yes."

"Please not yet."

He eased out.

She spun fast, threw her arms around his neck and opened his mouth with hers. A kiss – pervaded with tremors from the tease.

"You can still be hard and still save your explosion until tonight?"

"Yes."

"And save?"

"Yes. Women can finish many times for every one of a man. I think you know that now."

"Yes."

"I will take you today."

Jane did not say a word more, suddenly stunned by the risk, the peril of the fierce animal he might become. The wild buck running down the doe. It caught her breath.

"You're going to catch me and fuck me?"

"Yes."

By silent agreement, they dressed, he only in his buckskin breeches, she back in her riding skirt and blouse, missing a button each. He told her to wear nothing under.

"So you can ..."

He nodded.

They examined the stove. It was intended for use both as cooking station and to heat the three rooms of the house. Even though this August afternoon would be hot, they knew they would want a fire in the night. Hovey was able to judge the metal chimney safe after a climb on the roof to peer down it, and by a rag on a stick pushed up from the bottom. They kept water handy while starting a fire, to make sure it would draw and not catch on fire itself. And to cook.

Hovey made trail breakfast – bacon, eggs, bread toasted and buttered, coffee. They agreed it was fine, with bright eyes over the table.

12:25 p.m.

For no reason, Jane changed into a dress she had along. He had seen it once before, when she came to his room. It was white, yet abundantly flower-printed with red and orange blossoms, long, nearly brushing the floor when she swayed. She remarked with a pout that the dress was the only one to survive the Silver City flood and catastrophe.

They moved two old chairs onto the porch.

Small details of how they came to cross paths kept them amused. Life ironies. She told how she met the windmill expert, that this was the only time he could visit. Hovey reminded her how wrong it was to have a sign in the wild pointing to a woman. A woman with no rifle.

"I have something to tell you," she said.

"What."

"Four weeks from tomorrow, I will attend my first class of college."

"What?"

"I belong in college."

"There is none here."

"Yes, there is. It is new. This will be the second class, ever. It's called New Mexico Normal School. They are constructing a new building, so class is in the Presbyterian Church for a while, and they're getting ready for students now. Only 40 students. I am one. They accepted my admission."

Hovey listened in surprise. His intensity grew.

"This is college?"

"Yes. You must have a diploma from primary school, which I have from Ithaca. The Normal School is set up to train teachers of young children. I am in."

She explained that her enrollment was in the works for all of 1895, her uncle helping, paying Jane's tuition for the first year. She was required to promise she would teach in New Mexico on graduation.

"I almost gave it up last week. But now, just because a flood obliterated Main Street in Silver City, destroyed my uncle's store ... most of my clothes ... my keepsakes ...

nothing is going to stop me. Not even how to pay for food and rooming. Or books."

"I thought we had no secrets from each other."

Jane laughed at his joke. "You have never told me the name of the two other women you had, Hovey. Don't. Ever. That is your secret."

"This is impressive."

"It just never was the right time to tell you."

"What about this ranch?"

"I have to figure out where to live. Class is only three days a week for Normal School, Monday, Wednesday, and Thursday, we are supposed to do reading, writing, and study the other days. It's a seventy-minute ride from school to here. If I can find an inexpensive bed in town on three nights, I can live out here four nights. Or ... ride all the way in and back every school day. If Grey will stand for that!"

"Hmm, $55 for the windmill, no glass in the windows, not much firewood piled up, fences with falling-down posts ..."

"I can hand-pump the water. I've nailed canvas to the outside of the windows. The stove works."

He gazed out to the west.

"We will find out if the roof leaks. A storm is coming."

He asked Jane to show the deed for the ranch, which she had with her. He showed her the document granting the franchise to run cattle on the Gila.

There was a moment of silence as they stood on the porch in respect for two human beings with aspirations, plans, and grit to make them happen.

"But I want sex, Hovey."

"It is too far away."

"I'll just be the chaste and wholesome nineteen-year-old student, diligent and polite, but who rides out to her hidden ranch to meet a wild stallion smelling like the open range who ravishers her ten times over two days every month. Then she shows up on Monday in a modest frock to learn how to teach children to read."

They circled each other. Testing the heat between.

"Here I am, standing in a dress, all normal on my porch, but you'll be inside me again in a moment."

"Yes."

"Cock in me."

"Yes."

"Sometimes I like knowing how it's coming."

"I like entering."

"Tell me."

"Back against the railing. Lift the dress. Slow. Hem in your fingertips. Do the shy thing again, eyes down. That is put on, right?"

"I won't tell you."

"I like pretend shy. And real."

"I won't tell you. It might be real modesty to not look in your eyes, or I might be wild hungry but teasing shy."

He opened his britches. Yes, the cock jutted forth once more, and yes, she looked. At the thing. Erect. Pointing up. Gigantic to her coy self. She lifted the dress as ordered – hem taken in fingers, the flower-print fabric sliding up over thighs, abdomen, to the bottom of breasts. Jane quivered from the deliberate exposure of her nude hips and belly – and the provocative delta waiting. Hovey approached, stepped between her legs, crouched slightly, fit the head to lips, and penetrated her body. The thrust lifted her on tiptoes.

"Oh ..." she groaned.

She wiggled down, settling her weight at the root.
"Oh Sir, not again?"
"Yes."

Hovey eased out, then made one smooth stroke, leaving it pulsing inside her body. In a shock, she grasped the male drive with horrible immediacy.

It will always push in.
That's all it knows, blind, dumb – only
the mighty need to thrust through
soft flesh and seek the womb.

It stunned, realizing how fierce the cock needs.

Hovey kept the pressure. The *in* pressure. She breathed with him. Shy Girl did not look up.

He withdrew. A step back. She still held the hem of her flower dress in fingertips.

They froze in expectation. It lasted two, three, four breaths. Then ... she lifted her eyes to his. Carnal thoughts flashed from one to the other. Pleasure in it. Delicious and good.

She up-turned her head to fit the tilt of his.

Their mouths enclosed each other.

The kiss grew urgent. Wild with seeking. They did not press bodies together, making the fervor in the kiss run strong.

Jane slipped out, moved a few feet from Hovey, spun to face him. Now she lowered the hem of the dress. They stood in a quiet tableau.

Then, with bare feet padding on wood floors, she floated inside with the grace of a bemused dancer, a smile teasing invitation. She swayed around the room as if entranced by soft gaiety. Hovey watched from the doorway.

Her dance slowed next to the table. The old, dry,

prospector's table, huge, its thick oak top stained by spilled coffee, marked with damage from rough days long gone. Jane had cleaned it, treasured it, left it bare. Now she stood at its side, expressionless.

A moment in the warm afternoon reached fullness. Her body bent at the waist, torso descending to the tabletop, hands reaching across to grip the far edge. Her head lay still, turned away from the doorway and the man filling it.

Time reset by the gage of eros ascending – its weight conveyed in his approach, the arrival of his nakedness somewhere behind, the silence that set surety deep, his fingers brushing her leg at the calf as they took hold of the light garment terminating there.

The yearning that blossomed then, with the hem of cotton slipping up the back of thighs seeming to make strands of hair-filaments bend and spring loose, nearly causing her to squirm and cry out – but she did not. The hem stopped at the top of thighs, the dress taut over her bottom.

Hovey dragged the fabric up. The flesh of both cheeks shivered and bounced free.

Jane, exposed once more. She contained the thrill of it, not a sign outward, with the effect of something wonderful slowly ripening on the table.

In time, the hard organ penetrated the limpid one. No other parts of bodies touched. Measured quietude of breathing, keen pleasure of enjoyment, peace in it.

Hovey withdrew and backed away from the table. Jane, in love with the sensuous one-stroke takings, now begged him silently for the finish. Her erotic heart filled with greed for it, would burst unless he answered. Yet she did not signal. Absolute stillness and silence filled the room.

He stepped forward, pulled her erect, lifted the dress up and off in one motion, throwing it across the room. He spun her fast, lifted her off the floor and onto the table, pulling both legs up sharply, pinning knees adjacent her torso. Jane's arms wrapped around his neck and pulled him into place – his mouth buried in wet flesh between her thighs.

Hovey drank nectar then, as if finding it by a miracle on a petal in the desert. He was saved from death, for the flow of rich liquids sustained, proved a surfeit, and quelled his enormous thirst.

1:40 p.m.

Hovey woke.

He slipped from the bed and pulled on trousers. He paused to take in the sight of Jane's body, half-exposed, the long curve of leg mounting to the rise of hip, then falling nicely into the bend of narrow waist.

He glanced over to the old solid table, on which he had drunk deep, where his mouth on her wide-open sex had evoked riotous screams. The walls seemed still to send echoes of it. Subtle scent and taste of female liquids lay redolent on his mouth.

His next eruption hovered. All through the earlier teasing of single strokes, especially the one down into her throat, and then the greedy drinking at that table, he still held.

"All the more for later," he whispered, his eyes turning to her sleeping face.

Outside, he walked the perimeter. Odd, the arrangement of two parallel fences with four yards between. Why? Perhaps a dog run. The inner enclosure measured twenty yards across in a rough circle. On the east – to the left of the south-facing house – stood a bunkhouse, with lean-to attached to its north side. The two horses stood in it, tethered, since there was no swing-door on the building. He could not release them since the fences were down in many places. He led both to a small patch of poor prairie grass in a hollow and staked them. His horse needed a brush-down, and he set to. With the afternoon proceeding, a warming sun touched his back and lit the sandy sheen of the horse's flank. He confided in his mount.

"A man needs leave his woman behind to do his right work. To do out alone."

Will slowed his brushing. His head shook twice, slowly.

"But I would surely abide her at the end of such a day. Or once a month."

Investigating the bunkhouse, he found weathering outside, but no signs of sitting water damage outside or in. Perhaps the roof did not leak. The only furniture, a solid oak table – twin to the one in the ranch house – marked and weather-dry from age, and two pairs of stacked beds with no bedding.

He heard a step outside the door.

Jane entered wearing nothing but Hovey's shirt. Bare feet.

"Hovey …"

"Wear moccasins in this yard."

He yanked her into the middle of the room and wrapped her in full embrace.

"No, no, let me wake up first."

He closed his mouth over hers. They struggled inside the kiss. His hands roamed her body under the shirt. Jane clung to her sleepy resistance while thrilling to assault by aggressive hungry hands. She pulled her mouth away.

"Here it comes again ..."

"Yes." He lifted her off the floor, moved her to the closed door and crushed her against it with his weight. Her sex flooded in a surge. His trousers sank to the floor. His thighs forced hers apart. Jane absorbed the penetration like the piercing of armor for fatalistic death.

"Oh no no no I do not want to be fucked now."

Power like the cycles of steam engines descended upon her. *How can I be walking gently across the earth one moment, then be thrown under this train?* Wham, thud, in, in, in. A harsh grunt on each thrust.

She tried to spin around. He forced her to face front. She pushed against his chest. He slapped her hand away.

"Get off me."

He slammed in. The rod was thick and stiff. Rude. Her eyes flamed. She nearly spit in his face.

"You fuck me anytime you want?"

"Yes." He thrust harder. Her back thudded against the door.

"Not asking?"

"No."

"Fuck!" she screamed with ragged rage, trying to shrivel the cock. "Fuck!"

Abruptly her aspect flipped. Hips swayed to help his aim, head tilted down, face serene. Slowly, calmly, even while suffering every blow of rhythmic pounding, her arms lifted above her head, wrists crossed, to be caught by the imagined iron beam she could never defeat – but she loved it. Jane loved to be bound for sex. Each thrust jolted her body, which bounced back in place, ready to receive the next. She let poignant surrender fill her heart.

Into the storm, she whispered.

"... caught the sweet girl again, Hovey."

"Huh."

Jane's eyes would not allow his to catch.

"... tied her to a wall."

His thrusts pushed her body up the door.

"She's so soft like anything."

"Rhh, hunh, rnhh, rnhh, rnhh."

"Why do you fuck her so cruel?"

This enraged the cock. The swearing firecracker had vanished. This compliant thing infuriated. His thrusts, wilder. His grunting, loud.

"Hrm. Hrrm. Huh."

"... poor vagina, cock fucking it so rude."

"Rhh, hunh, hunh."

"She might like it a little ..." Jane squeezed her muscles around the rampaging organ. She tilted and swayed hips like a shameless temple dancer to accept it, to caress it, to make his pleasure flow. Harem girl.

She refused to meet his eyes with hers.

"Innocent young girl, ruined." She sighed and fluttered eyelashes.

Hovey slowed his effort. His right hand joined below. Fingers slid into place around the lips. The edge of his thumb fit against the hooded bud, caressing with fingers while forcing the rigid phallus deep.

"No no no. That is naughty."

Jane tried to remain a shy sex girl. But Hovey's fingers were too smart. The power of his penetrations too awful. She could not hide the start of her ride up.

"Oh no you don't."

She fought the urge to release her bound hands, to fight. More liquids flowed now.

"Oh. Oh. Not. Fair. Not. Fair. Huhn. Huhhn."

Hovey pulled out, came half around his captive, pushed the wet prick against her right thigh, thrust his hand deep into the vee, penetrating the orifice with two fingers as deep as nature would allow.

"Oh fuck fucking nooo."

The tips of his fingers sought the ripe spot on the inside-underside, on the roof of her vagina. He caressed it mercilessly, with thumb rubbing on the gland outside. She nearly collapsed. The hand buried in her sex held her up.

"Ho no oh ohohoh."

Jane never looked in his eyes. She never dropped her hands from the wall above her. She never avoided the pleasure coming fast. Her limbs shivered with sensation. His fingers moved fast now, her organs swollen, capable of accepting rude arousal from the aggressive, relentless hand.

"No no no no no!"

Another finger joined the two inside. They were greedy. She gulped a gigantic breath and held, his penetration so strong it seemed the hand gripped her womb itself. Fingertips caressed the magic spot with no mercy. It pulled her over the top. Every muscle in her pelvis seized ...

"Oohhhhhh!"

... and released a grand-bel explosion. Jane's juice flew everywhere. She gathered a breath full of fire, letting it go. It ripped her open.

"Nohhhh."

Hovey caressed between her thighs with no mercy, finding every scintilla of pleasure, then slowed to ease her down, his hand drenched, puddles of juice near her bare feet. Jane's body jerked with pulsations – a woman undone yet again, helpless, melted, ecstatic.

Thrilling, letting herself remain bound and tied to the wall while shaking with pleasure, knowing the bindings held only because she let them. Several minutes passed until her breathing settled and she could speak.

"My arms are worn out. You should use real rope."

He slapped his left hand on her wrists to pin them. His right-hand fingers remained inside her sex. Now, finally, she looked him in the eye.

"You like me shy and demure when bound by ropes."

"Yes."

"Or fighting mad."

"Yes."

"What did you do to me?" There was a stream of juice down her leg.

"You were ready for that, for that place inside to let loose. Fingers are better than cock to find it. It makes waters." He caressed the spot inside.

"I nearly fainted. I still might."

"I will catch you. I can do it to you again. Now." He increased the pressure of his touch.

Jane felt eager new arousal blossom under his hand. He was right – she could race to the finish again immediately.

"I dare you to see my freedom, even with your ropes around me."

It took Hovey several seconds to understand her poetry, then to agree, in his silent way.

"Take both hands away," she ordered. He dropped the left from her wrists and withdrew the right from the warm cave. Their bodies touched nowhere.

She lowered her arms to her side and pressed both

hands against the wall. An aftershock tremor rippled her pelvis.

"Wait ..." she said, hooded eyes looking into the void. Another sweet contraction. She breathed into it to run the pleasure deep.

"I love that," she whispered. "Like a wave right through me."

"Yes."

"They say earthquakes have shocks for days after."

"Yes. I felt one once."

She held for the next one, a delicious quiver through. Three long breaths to taste it.

"I am still bound."

He nodded.

"Almost kiss me."

Hands on the door on either side of her shoulders, he leaned in. Their mouths hovered within an inch. They rotated to make a phantom kiss. Jane ached to have lips touching. She nearly always ached for that.

"You were gone for ten days," she whispered. "Did you dream of my mouth?"

"Yes."

"Dream of kissing it?"

"Yes."

"Say what Marguerite told you."

"Breathe her breath. Drink the honey she offers on her tongue."

"Kiss me."

Neither required warming. They touched nowhere except at the blending of lips. Each took the other's syrup. They swam in it for minutes, simple and sweet one moment, wild and voracious the next. It became the slightest pressing, closed, then changed to deep searching, uninhibited. Most arousing – the sliding of lips around tongue. Each around each, in time.

Jane's sex glowed – it seemed directly connected to her mouth. Can a kiss liquify everything between a woman's legs?

She pulled out of kissing him. They stared at each other silently.

"I am bound, my hands are tied to the wall. But do what I say."

He did not agree – in his wordless way.

She waited, enrobed with his shirt on her naked body, savoring the luscious kiss, redolent with softness of sugar perfumed with his wet insides. Her clitoris still thrummed, having been rubbed into infinity just before.

"If you won't do what I say, I'll use 'stop' to turn off sex."

"You want the finish. I am holding."

"You taught me to touch myself, Hovey. I can finish anytime. Now let me be boss for five minutes."

"It is not the same as taking you. I favor that way."

"I noticed."

"You crave to be taken, Jane."

In the pause, her eyes admitted it. Yet she insisted ...

"Let me be boss."

He nodded.

"I wish we had real rope here. To bind my wrists behind." She moved them to the small of her back, fitted between the wall and her body. "But they are truly tied. I can't get loose."

He nodded.

Then, Jane stepped forward, transformed. Defiant Girl and Demure Girl were gone. Her stance took on the stature of a Greek goddess, upright, forward, solid on the earth. In her clear face, the pride of womanhood. She wore the after-flush of orgasm on it.

"Unbutton the shirt."

As he undid the buttons, sparks flew as he eased the shirt off her shoulders and over bare breasts. These seemed to dominate attention as he loosed the final buttons.

"Be sure the shirt is tight at the wrists. Make a binding behind."

He used the material, winding it around in back, and indeed she could not slip out at the wrists. She was securely bound with his shirt. Otherwise – naked. The warming afternoon and the aftermath of sex left her skin glowing, shining with a sheen of sweat.

Jane moved away. Increasing the drama of her proud attitude, she visited every corner of the bunkhouse as if surveying her lands. The binding contributed, pulling her shoulders back, thrusting her chest ahead on each step.

"I own this room."

Hovey stood in admiration. Fascination. She turned her attention on him, the appraisal starting and ending at his semi-erect sex, gloating over it. She owned this too.

"Open the door."

Hovey donned britches, snapped suspenders over torso, slipped into boots, and followed her out to the yard fronting the bunkhouse. They felt the elevated heat and remarked on oncoming storm clouds advancing from the northwest over Los Pinos Altos range.

"Why must you still be tied?"

"This is correct, for women. We are bound in this world."

He did not respond – she did not explain.

"You have to wear something in this yard, Jane.

Moccasins or boots."

"I own this ground – I will tread it with bare feet."

"Scorpions. And cactus needles."

"Then carry me to my house."

He lifted her in his arms. She did not snuggle into the corner of them, rather rode the ride as if on a mount. He ascended the stairs and set her down on the porch. She strolled its perimeter, head held high, arms bound behind, surveying her property, the ominous clouds in the west, and her warrior-stallion with the dark brown hair and strong arms – and a battle scar across his body.

"You are walking like a queen," he said.

"I attended a play, an opera, in Santa Fe once, and the queen in it ... you could not remove your eyes. I wanted to be her."

"You are."

"All women should walk like this after sex."

"People would notice."

"Also, when she wants sex. To tell the man."

She floated into the ranch house. Again, a promenade.

"I own this room."

Jane's dreamlike state deepened. It was a delirium, with nothing of it thought untrue. Its surreality was so compelling, Hovey joined her. She halted six feet from him, and her appraisal of his person resumed. She assessed the situation right through his pants.

"The manly thing?"

"Yes?"

"It goes up and down."

"Yes. Resting now."

"I wish it to awake."

"Say something."

"The queen adores it. She burns to possess it and

command it. To cause its ... erectness. Then she desires to bathe it with her juices. All her juices."

"Whose manly thing?"

"Her consort. The one she calls into her bed when she wants sex. He must not wither or expend, no matter what she does to it. With it. He must stay hard as a tree until she screams her last scream. Hard cock until she is satisfied."

"Does her ... consort ... know how to not finish?"

"They have engaged many times, but now the queen wishes a new way. She wishes to achieve many times in one evening. He is sometimes too impatient with his explosion."

"How can he learn?"

"She could send her young maid ahead, to train him how to hold his finishing."

"Why is she sending her maid? The queen could do it better."

"She wants him trained ahead. Also ... to give her favorite lady a treat."

"What would the girl say?"

"The queen has sent me to lie with you. Did she warn you?"

"Yes."

"I am not the queen, yet I know what she wants during your trysts with her."

The ridiculous word 'tryst' made Jane and Hovey fall out of their pretend. They realized the gift of poetry her parents bequeathed had awakened. Jane made him remove the shirt binding her wrists behind her back. She pretended to don an elaborate dress of the court and visit him in chambers. They jumped back in the game.

"What is your name?" he asked.

"Anne."

"Anne, remove your clothing. I want to see you naked."

"Sir, the queen told me to not take orders from you. I am to order you."

"Oh."

"If you give me another order, I am to whack you on your backside."

"No!"

"And we are not to kiss on the mouth. Do not."

"Oh."

"That is only for the queen."

"Hmmm."

"Remove your clothing. I wish to see you naked."

Hovey stripped.

"Oh oh," Anne said, "it is as she promised. Prodigious and prideful."

"It is difficult for me not to order you."

"Well, Sir, that is the gist of our bedding. I am to provoke you hard, keep you hard, you are to stay hard, and you shall not expend."

"The queen wants me –"

"To not expend. Do not."

She knelt on the floor in front of him. "Do not thrust. It is for me to make the impaling."

Anne took the consort's manly thing into her mouth.

In sure slow rhythm, glancing up with coquetry when drawing off, eyes shut when pressing forward, she engulfed the cock with the enthusiasm of a lusty wench. She swirled her hand around the shaft, letting wet from her mouth lubricate. She seemed to have no lack of this, nor hesitation to let it drench her hand and his organ. The slushing sound incited them both.

"Am I pleasing?"

"Yes," he grunted. "Yes."

"It is delicious in my mouth. I will suck it for hours."

She resumed her oral laving and lapping. Dutifully, she engaged all her skill, tried hard to bring him off, took him to the edge three times, then removed the furious thing, tilted her head up, separated her lips just so, and invited him to gaze into her mouth. She steadied and swayed to be sure he could see deep – deep into the fully surrendered cave, luscious with liquids. That was so arousing, he had to look away after a moment. When he returned to attention, she increased the heat in her visage.

"I bathe you in my juice here," she said, hand under her chin, fingers around her neck, "because it thrills my quim. When cock slides in here, it makes honey on the lips twixt my thighs."

Hovey wobbled with the earthy words.

"And the queen no less so. She is abundantly wet."

"Yes?"

"Yes." The phallus twitched in her hand. "Oh, you want to spurt off now." She opened her mouth to him again, exposing the depth of it. Her eyes glistened. "To fill me to overflowing. All over my lips and tongue. Do you wish?"

"Yes."

Smiling, she slowly shook her head.

"No. You will not."

She took the tip between her lips. They fit over it, barely touching. She washed it in the slippery liquor that filled her mouth. Easing forward, the shaft penetrated halfway. She held everything in watery suspension. Then, with melted sensuality, she arched her head forward and took the cock to its root.

"Oh fuck," moaned the consort.

She slid back, gathered her breath, and eased forward to make cock slish magically smooth, deep into her throat again.

"Yah. Yah yah yah." His hips trembled from so full a devouring.

She did not struggle – except to let it go deeper. Nothing had ever been this bold, to penetrate and stay buried. When the forbidden finishing contractions threatened to defeat the game, she withdrew. He did not expend.

Anne had magically become naked from the courtly dress in which she had arrived, and some juice now fell to her breasts. She touched here and there, spreading wet to her nipples. She smiled wickedly up into his eyes.

"I have never taken a man that deep. Ever. It went right down in ... I don't know how far. Forever far. You provoke me to wantonness."

"Your mouth ..."

"The queen's is better."

"Really?"

"We bantered about it once ... who can accommodate the deepest. I defer to her proficiency. She is queen."

"May I ask for something?"

"Yes, you may ask, but do not dare to order me."

"Would you do it again?"

"Yes, sire."

In her being, she treasured her position on her knees before the queen's man. She offered him the sight of her mouth again, open, glistening, pink. Then she slipped it over the tip of the erect cock. Her lips fit under the rim, swayed there, while her mouth filled with wet again. Bathing. Savoring. She imagined this living ball of flesh

soon to press the womb-opening of her queen. She
wanted it to touch hers.

She eased him in, pillowing the shaft on her tongue.
With eyes closed, movements settling, "Jane" came to the
surface and nearly overwhelmed her fun persona as Anne.
A threat of sin hovered, unnatural sin, for taking a man
this way. Cock in her mouth – and its emission. But then
a quiver in her pelvis, a surge of blessing. She eased her
head forward, allowed the shaft to slip in, to pass
resistance, to slide firmly home with the tip imbedded in
her throat.

"Rhghah ..." the consort snorted.

She was impudent Anne once more. She fit her hands
around his low back and pulled his body forward. One,
two, three beats of time – her heart filled with goodness.
She drew off the cock. It sprung free, red, glistening.
Gasping for air, she smiled up at him with shining eyes,
licking her lips.

"God's design of our bodies prevents me from having
you deeper, sir."

"You are a wicked fox, miss."

"It is so proud and thick, it thrills to have it deep. I
adore it deep."

"Wicked shameless angel."

"Do you wish your cock down my throat ten more
times?"

"Yes!"

"No."

She stood. A moment – she almost kissed his mouth.
Quickly she turned away, padded to the side of the bed.
Without looking back, she gestured with her hand for
him to approach. Gaining composure, she ordered him to
lie prone, face up. The organ of manliness was certainly

ready for engagement.

"Remember, you are not to expend. This will be your test. To watch me exhaust myself on you while I use it like the rod of heaven, to reach my end. You are not to spurt out."

"The queen lets you finish with me?"

"She demands it. She needs you to restrain when I fly to the sky and shower your belly with juice. I surely have abundant juice. When I come off, I will be screaming. I will squeeze so tight you will beg with your soul to shoot up into me. Do not."

"May I thrust?"

"No. Stay hard as the trunk of a tree. That is all."

"Oh."

"I will report your restraint to the queen. If you restrain. And stay hard."

Anne climbed on the bed, crouched above his body, and lowered her sex onto the phallus, her weight jamming it home. Her strong pelvis took charge. She rocked. She slid. Her fingers stroking the button atop the lips of the yoni made honey flow from within and bathed it slick. Sweat flung off her body as she twisted on the rigid pole. She squealed with joy, spluttering nonsense, one shout on each descent.

"Pradz. Prad. Szod. Shing. Szhing. Zhing!"

Looking down, she thrilled to see fat lips pushed aside by each thrust, the shaft gleaming. She gripped it each time it disappeared into her flesh, making the squashing sound of ripe fruit mashed to jam. Exotic scents rose above the bed.

"Frmp. Frrig. Huh. Huh. Ha."

She wedged her hands on his chest for more leverage. Shaking her head like a wild she-lion, drops of sweat

slashed across his body. Seeming never to tire, set free by
royal permission, unafraid to let carnal fire rage, Anne
stroked relentlessly, perhaps a hundred strokes, perhaps
desperate to kill a knot in her belly, and that would set the
queen free.

He circled her neck with one hand. Their eyes locked.
She increased her ride, the constriction around cock and
ferocity of intent – the intent to pull his organ out by the
root. His grip on her neck suggested they would die
together if she did.

"Fuck. Fuck ..." she spouted.

"Yes."

"Fuck."

"Yes."

"Fuck!"

He released his hold on her neck. His hand sought the
vee and found the gland pulled into erection by the
shaft's passage. He twitched it brazenly.

She inhaled a great breath, eyes wide open. Her young
body froze above him, only the tip of the phallus between
lips. Jane on the edge of glory.

A thudding splash down. All seized between her
fluttering thighs.

"Yhahah!"

"Yes."

"Nhahah."

Anne crashed down onto his body, moaning, crying,
laughing, shuddering. Her liquids combined with drops
from the humid air and the scents of their bodies. Carnal
realities and soaring delight suffused her mind and soul.

"A woman's greatest achievement," he said.

She could not speak. The after-quakes began.

2:35 p.m.

The August afternoon had reached the peak of Southwestern heat. They lay pressed together in its steam. She asserted her weight on him, squirming, laughing, body drenched and heaving, sliding her breasts against his chest to mix her sweat with his. The sheen on skin combined with a pool of liquids that had overflowed. Her dark hair had turned darker from exertion, soaked. She did not lift off – he did not diminish in hardness. Her satisfaction included awareness of a considerable erection embedded in a small vagina. All awaited the next drama.

"Sir?"

"Yes?"

"The queen ordered one last thing."

"Yes?"

"I am to find the joy again. I know I can do it, my tender parts still throb for it, can you feel?" She contracted around his organ.

"Yes." He spread his hands on her bottom and pulled and squished the globes while she renewed the power of her inner muscles.

Anne shrieked with delight. "Oh sir!"

She looked right in his eyes.

"But you are to be the engine this time. You must fuck me with all your strength and might, until I am delirious with pleasure."

He rose on the bed, flipped her over, dropped her body onto the mattress. His thighs forced hers apart. His hand guided the shaft, the tip making one swish to open the orifice. He loosed full weight into the plunge. It rippled her insides as it went home.

"Oh no no no no no."

The cock emerged. His hands fit behind her knees and

pushed her legs high until the tops of thighs lay flat on the bed, pinning her down. The lips and orifice rose into limpid vulnerability and exposure.

Before he could thrust, she spoke.

"Fuck my cunt until I faint."

3:24 p.m.

"Look at this."

Jane pulled away some debris behind the water reservoir to reveal a good-sized iron bathtub with ornate feet and brass fixtures, standing solid on a slatted platform, smooth white porcelain inside. Hovey remarked that the long conduit lying in the dust next to it had once enabled filling of the tub directly from the reservoir.

She found a stopper for the drain.

"This would take some pumping," he said.

They stood for a moment, each of them sweating profusely, miserable, even if a major storm declared its imminent arrival by dark clouds marching in from the west, even if immoderate sex in the August West had caused the sweat. They wanted a bath.

"I am the boss of this ranch. And everyone in it. Fill it."

"We will take turns."

Fifteen minutes later the tub was three-quarters full from hand-pumping the well, and they were even more drenched with perspiration. Hovey seemed dazed, Jane delighted. She plunged in.

"Golly yikes!" she screamed. Cold by contrast.

Hovey did not make a sound as he sunk down. He went still, staring at her face with sober expression.

"Jane?"

"Yes?"

"You are not the queen or Anne now?"

"No, I am Jane."

"That was almost a splendid moment of my life."

She laughed gaily. "Because you did not 'expend'?"

"Yes. I think you could be an actor."

"Thank you for joining the performance. I think I might be a poet." Her expression softened. "Forget about 'saving,' Hovey. Be done with that. Your will must not be my will. It must be free. Let it loose as needs."

"I was just about to declare that anyway."

"Oh."

"Where did you learn that one word?"

"Some of the other women washing for the hotel say it. That was the first time I ever said it. Anne would enjoy saying it."

"Call forth the queen for a moment."

"I am here."

"Thank you for sending your maid to me."

"She pleased?"

"Yes. Anne is wanton. She admitted it."

"I know that is true, from her sister-maids' gossip and one of my soldiers."

"He is lucky."

"How close did you come?"

"I almost shot off in her mouth, twice."

"I believe it."

"How old is she?"

"Nineteen."

"How did she learn?"

"A wild man of the forest, a hunter, abducted her from her horrid life in London and made her his sex slave.

I rescued her from that."

"She has great skill. Shows her lust for sex with pride."

"Yes. Anne told me all that happened. You passed the test. Retained your seed even though you plowed her like a wild beast."

Suddenly Jane saw his gaze fixed a foot below her chin.

"Hey!" she shouted, sinking to the neck with a splash. "Gawking at a lady like that ..."

He did not blink. She sank underwater, sputtered back up. Put on the coquette. A teasing smile. Her hands gathered the black tresses, squeezed the water from them, and twined them in place on top of her head. The uplift from this ballet brought the fascinating parts back into view. She pretended not to notice the focus of his eyes.

Parts needed washing. Slippery parts. An innocent girl tending to her cleanliness in a matter-of-fact manner, with a bar of soap she had brought to the wilderness. Her hands also roamed shoulders, neck, and – with arms raised high one at a time – the hollows under.

Without looking at him, Jane slid her left foot across under water. It discovered something soft. Her toes plied it gently. The stoic person to whom it belonged grunted in surprise.

"Brumpft!"

Jane pretended not to hear a thing, as if nothing were occurring beneath the waves. He shifted to give her toes a better angle.

Gradually, the caressing of her breasts became no longer functional. Hands slowed, circled, lifted. Her eyes rose, and from beneath soft lashes sought his.

"I always hope you'll kiss them, then my mouth, then them, then my mouth, until I weep."

"I will do that, many times."

"If you disremember, I'll start yelling, 'I'm a nineteen-year-old girl with beautiful breasts, now get over here and kiss them'."

"I would."

"I could finish with such kissing. I believe. When your lips pull at the tips, it shoots right down between my legs. I could finish –"

"Jane?"

"I am here."

"The queen's consort is the king."

Her head jerked to his. Her hands slashed the water. She vaulted out of the bathtub, slipped into moccasins, and bolted to the porch of the house. She looked back to see him striding with purpose.

Jane ran inside. She halted with back to the table, hands gripping its edge, breathing hard. She tracked Hovey as he entered and approached, then took two steps forward and held her ground, elongating her stance, donning the dignity of a naked monarch standing forthright before her potent mate. Most water had been flung from her body, but she shook her head violently, so her hair rained drops across the floor. She kicked off the moccasins.

He must expend now.

The illusion of queen returned, more vivid than ever. She clung to it, imagining the future of the kingdom at stake.

"Then give me a princess."

Hovey took her in his arms, lifted her as if nothing, carried her to the bed. Gently, tenderly, he settled her down, all grace befitting. She opened her arms to him. As he entered the embrace, her thighs parted, all desire befitting.

Their bodies joined at the nexus of man and woman. All passion befitting.

Not another word spoken. Only eyes holding eyes, linked deep. To the rhythm of his hips rocking, her sorrows rose like blood flowing from wounds. Yet her joys twined around the pain, and healed.

Jane's heart believed she would bring no child into this dusty world. Nonetheless, she dared indulge the queen's craving for a daughter, with a prince to follow.

As Hovey reached his end, moaning with release, she imagined the poem of the queen. It tore truth from the ragged remains of her innocence.

Come above me. Come between my thighs. Part the lips. Open the sheath, my vagina. Penetrate me. Use all your manliness to make me explode, so my birthing muscles pull the juice from you. My eager cunt will quiver and seize, dipping the cervix into the lake, urging the seed into my womb. Plant a baby so deep in my body I become the mother of everything. My breasts will fill, and I will nourish the world, with your lips around the tips first.

We will save the realm.

j.j.kirnan

part 5
august 1895

profound as the midnight sea

August 11, 1895
Sunday
Seven miles east of Silver City, NM

4:11 p.m.
Rain approached.

They stood on the porch, remaining naked to tolerate the oppressive heat and humidity, knowing it would be washed away by the coming storm. Although eager when Hovey's powerful body moved toward her with intent, Jane delighted in the nearness of sex, while not having to – her pelvis warm with the serenity of queenly satisfaction.

"From now on I'll always do that every month the days before my flow. When it's safe."

"What?"

"Invite the king to fill me, so I'm with child."

Prior, Jane had remembered the words of the queen's poem-prayer. She wrote them in her journal.

"So we can save the realm."

"What about the rest of the month?"

"Finish finish finish."

He laughed. A rare thing.

"You like it, Hovey."

"What?"

"To make a woman foolish for sex."

"I do not make you. You are a fool for it on your own."

Jane's expression admitted it. She gave him credit, anyway, for fun.

"And you are the fastest to finish of any woman in the world."

"I learned a different word for it," she said.

"You did?"

"Orgasm."

"I heard that once."

"I did some research on sex while you were gone, cowboy."

"You did?"

"I found a book called Gray's Anatomy. It had pictures. And descriptions. And another book about 'how.' Not a virgin anymore, so I have to read up on things. College girl, studying her subject."

"I never learned sex in a book. Maybe I missed something."

"Hovey, you don't hate talking with a woman, you like to kiss, you care about my pleasure, you teach me to touch myself, you find the sweet spot inside my vagina, you play sex imagination with me so we can rule the world, you withhold your orgasm even with the manly thing thrust up inside the wild vagina of a wild child, letting me finish so many times. You even let me say 'vagina' as many times as I want."

"Yes."

"Vagina."

"Yes."

"Does any other man out there know you are like that? You must be some kind of saint."

"No. I am not a saint. I am a cowboy."

"My cowboy."

"Normally, I would forbid you to call me cowboy. But now I am one."

"Why did you take this?"

"Cannot make a living any more providing the army and the copper mines with game. Not even bison. They want beef. They pay higher for beef than game."

"Oh."

"I will sell this herd in one shot to the army quartermaster."

"Do you know how to manage a herd?"

"Yes. Ran one in Texas. Small."

"How did you get the scar, Hovey?"

His eyes jerked to hers. She stared at him, deadpan.

"Witchy woman."

Jane did not flinch.

Hovey stood up straight. He looked away, then looked right in her eyes.

"I killed two men. The second one almost killed me."

Naked in the drenching heat, with the first sound of thunder off in the west, Hovey told the tale. How he left the herd for five hours one day, with a cowhand as watch guard. Another herder, with evil reputation, had been scouting Hovey's thirty-seven cows with greed, designing a brand that could be made by overlaying Hovey's. Seeing him depart, thinking it was Hovey's once-a-week overnight absence, he ambushed the cowhand, tied him up, and began rebranding.

"When I returned, half a mile out I could see something wrong. I carry a glass, and I saw this person in among my animals through it. I circled in behind and surprised him flat footed, rifle ten feet from his hand. He started after it. I shouted I had the drop on him, shouted for him to stop, put a shot in the ground near his gun."

"Oh..."

"I had to put a bullet in his chest, Jane. He got one shot off before he died. It just missed me."

"Oh Hovey ..."

"I did not account for the other. He had gone for firewood without his gun, but he charged me from behind. I spun just in time, but his knife went an inch in my belly, and then sliced like you see, right across and up my side. I have never felt pain like that. Horrible. I could not bring rifle to bear, but I got my hand on a rock, and when he charged with the knife ..."

He hesitated.

"Say it."

"I bashed his face in. They say a shard of his cheekbone cut through his brain."

"How did you survive?"

"So much blood, but the knife did not cut any big veins. Cowboy was only fifty feet away, tied up. I cut the ropes just before I passed out."

Jane walked across the porch. He did not follow. She glanced back at him, then out into the west, where dark clouds continued their approach. An impulse to cover her nakedness – refused, to show courage.

"Did you ever kill anyone else, Hovey?"

"Yes."

"Tell me. Tell everything." She walked back to face him.

"Whiskey. Money. Arguing. Insult. I turned my back to walk away from it. He struck me from the blindside with a chair and grabbed a heavy leg of it when it shattered, to strike, but I landed a punch, and his head hit a stone stair. Dead as he lay."

"In New York that would be manslaughter."

"There was a trial. Lucky, one other person saw the fight. She liked me more than the other."

"Did you bed her before or after the trial?"

"Both. The judge did not find that out. He called it self-defense. Because I had walked away, and he was set to kill me with that club. It had nails sticking out. That man had done near-murder twice before, escaped that very judge's intent to hang him both times."

"She was one of the two women you had before me."

"Yes."

"Do not tell me her name. Do not ever tell me."

"Are you afraid of me now?"

"Yes."

"Do you like it?"

"No."

Only half true and only half false.

"The two women ... whom I will not name?"

"Yes?"

"Both of them died, Jane."

"Oh my God."

"While I was away on the trail."

"They had promised themselves to you?"

"Yes."

"What happened?"

"In Laredo. Her horse pulled up for a rattler. She went over his head. She was dead from a broken neck before she stopped rolling."

"The other?"

"She left me, Jane. Went East to collect an inheritance and a house. There was a fire."

She stared at him with big eyes, stunned. It was clear he had loved both women.

"Oh, Hovey."

"I might have more rage than you."

"Oh."

"There is more."

"Hovey, do not stop until I hear everything. Everything."

"Three hangings, I was right on top of. On a jury for

one. A witness on another, an evil person who killed two miners just to get a bag of gold."

"And the last one?"

"A man who killed a friend of mine. People had to block me from taking that situation into my own hands. I am still raging on that today, Jane. We grew up together, Ramon and I."

"What else?"

"I am only twenty-four, but I have been around so much death and killing. I might have killed five-hundred large animals."

"If you didn't, someone else would."

"People cannot live on oats."

"No, they can't."

She paused to absorb. Her next words came with quiet pathos.

"This is the West."

He nodded. "But I have bad fate all around me. Did you feel it in your hand when you put it on my chest that morning?"

"No. It felt right."

"Do you want your heart near my dark fates?"

"If it will make you learn you have nothing bad about you."

"I could drag you down."

"No, you won't, William Bennis Hovey. I am stronger than you."

"Never pity me, Jane."

"I will proud you."

Hovey stopped solid. A jolt in his eyes. Jane wore bright certainty of her words in her open face.

"Were the hangings fair?"

"Yes."

"Were your three killings fair?"

"Yes."

"What about two women dying on you?"

"I have bad fate all around me. You will know that now."

"Well, this is fucking awful."

He burst out laughing. "You have started using that word for bad things."

"Fuck!"

He laughed again, with more mirth than Jane had heard in their time together. Healing floated on the porch. They might have thinned out the darkness. Jane felt inside for her happiness. There. Alive. Bruised, not killed. She put her body against her man. They held each other without pity for sorrow, while the rain began to pelt the yard, splashing in dust to make ripples, as if teardrops in the ocean.

4:45

It rained with conviction. Jane and Hovey dressed, chatting and joking, relieved to feel the heat and humidity flee before the storm.

His eyes followed her as she donned the flower-print dress, a step forward as it slipped down her body. She knew his present slight smiles with lit-up eyes were an exception – Hovey was not a gregarious man. While she adored his solid countenance – stoic as cactus – even more the delight to make it shatter by her wit. That would serve them well.

Jane started beans simmering gently, the first step of their ham dinner to come. Rain rattled the roof. They checked the walls and ceiling joints for leakage, agreeing it was a miracle to not find trouble, given the abandon of the place for so long. Satisfied, they settled into the two chairs on the porch to watch the downpour. Thunder rumbled, and flashes of lightning came closer. At the height of the storm, they made a promenade of the porch, awed by nature, gaudy in display.

"I have spent my life outdoors," he said. "Many storms like this."

"Me, none, little. And now I might be a homesteader with dust blowing into my house. Another part of my past dismissed, the bookish girl who stays inside to read. I like her, but I want to destroy her life and start over, and let the books come back one by one."

When he did not answer, she realized he had disappeared inside the ranch house. She turned to watch for the next lightning strike.

"Here. Shoot it."

She spun around. Hovey stood with arm outstretched holding his rifle.

"No!"

"Shoot the old."

She grabbed the rifle with attitude, pointed it in the general direction of reality, and pulled the trigger. No one knows where the bullet went.

"I want to kill something," she said, face grim. She took three wild pot shots into the rain.

This needed instruction. Hovey took a step to come behind her. He taught her how to reload.

"I might be arming the most dangerous person in New Mexico," he said under his breath.

6:10 pm

A happy dinner. Rich bean and ham soup with onions and carrots, some greens thrown in. Cheese and bread. They made it a feast by attitude, without wine, beer, or whiskey. At the end, both pulled chocolate bars from hiding, resulting in delight both delectable and ironic.

"This might make kissing better," she said, a shard of a bar melting on her tongue.

They leaned toward each other for discovery. Jane let Hovey search for sweet chocolate liquids under her lips. And deeper.

"That's what it is for," she said when they drew apart. "God made chocolate for that."

"You do not have God, Jane."

She kissed him again.

Eventually, he rose to evaluate the condition of firewood and kindling. Dark would fall in two hours, and with the blanket of humidity chased away by the storm, fire would be needed, even if it were August.

Jane finished clearing the table. She seemed to take particular pleasure wiping it clean, her hand lingering on the wood with a final swish-away of a crumb. This solid old table held new history now, being well-used for two fine meals – and one carnal feast. She stood upright and quiet, one hand's fingers resting on the tabletop, eyes on Hovey as he concluded his task.

He saw her attentive gaze. "What is it, Jane Whitfield?"

Jane marked the moment, still and serious.

"You've never told anyone how you live with all those deaths."

"No."

"I never told anyone about living with mine."

"No."

"I thought it was my fate to be in pain forever."

"Do you still?"

"No! Something's making me silly!"

She expected he would laugh. He only nodded.

"We must have felt pleasure coming to us, Hovey. The pain must out. Our violent pleasures have come to wash it away."

"You would have sex for that?"

"Yes. With you. I'm not letting you out of my sight until I finish so many times, I'm a new woman. Free."

"You think I would have sex for that?"

"Yes. Finishing in the body of a woman gives you peace. For a while."

He came close, bringing his strength along.

"Marguerite warned me about you."

Jane giggled. "She did?"

"She said I would meet you some day."

"What did she say?"

"'A woman instantly inside the walls of your hard heart'."

"That's right."

"'She will walk right through'."

"Yes."

Jane glowed to be this girl.

"Marguerite said, 'If you make love to her, you will not rid yourself of her easily. Or ever'."

"Never."

"Why did you offer yourself that first morning, Jane?"

"I knew there would be something softer ... wait, no ... I knew there would be something much harder than your heart waiting for me."

Hovey's eyes went sharp, then wide. Then, they both erupted in a roaring laugh. Jane preened with victory of her upside-down poetry. Her eyes shone wet and glinting with it.

Hovey moved.

"Stop!" The first time she had used her protective word. He froze, a smile in place. Jane believed it would be impossible for anything to 'stop' this man – except by agreement. Hovey looked completely different with a smile. "Stay there, until I call you near."

Amused, Hovey stood against the opposite side of the table, upright and strong, eyes alive with challenge.

She shifted her hips. Now the cove between her thighs fit the corner of the massive table.

"I want to finish so many times, Hovey. To throw off the damn shade. To be proud to chase it down the street."

Hovey nodded.

"I love this table."

The corner of it did not budge as her body melted into the edge. A person could rely on it to be hard forever.

"You didn't run from the bed when I told you my troubles and wept so long that first night."

"No."

"You looked right in my eyes when I touched myself the first time and brought pleasure."

"Yes."

"I couldn't hold your aspect perfectly."

"You did well."

A quick flick of the hips and a shudder ran through the table. With subtle tilting and swivel of pelvis, Jane's face began to flush. Her speaking slowed, halting with sensation.

"I want ... to show you again. With eyes open, Hovey. Will you look in?" A sharp indrawn breath with every sway of hips. "Because ... you are not afraid to look. Will you hold ... and stay right there?"

"Yes."

She pressed forward. A sweet 'oh' of pleasure escaped. With grace, Jane grasped the hem of the flower-print dress. Between presses against the wood, she inched it higher. It passed the level of the tabletop. The uncovered nether lips wedged into the corner-edge. Her voice grew thick, ardent with goodness.

"Oh. Oh."

Hovey did not look down. It sent Jane racing high into arousal – a matching dare from a man, to see sex in the eyes of the other. She tugged the dress off and tossed it on the floor. Hovey yanked off his shirt and dropped it on the dress. As the rocking settled into rhythm, her hand joined the excitement below, its fingers guiding the bud, the lips, even the inside flesh against the wooden edge. Soon she needed only the swirl of hips against the table to increase the fire.

"Oh, mm, yes. Yes."

Glancing down, her hands rose and caressed up her abdomen. Her gaze elevated. When she slipped both hands under breasts, she again locked eyes with Hovey, even when her hands sinuously cradled and shaped the flesh. The rocking of tender parts against the corner of the table grew urgent.

"Uhng, uhn, oh, unhng..."

Soon it was difficult to keep her eyes on his, so swift the rise. Yet she did. Hovey did not falter, four feet away at the other side of the table – he did not look down, he did not look away – again the cruel tenderness of an ennobled man of the West such as he, keeping his promise. The edifice of his being swelled in her heart – a man, steadfast and firm, perfect for her to savage against and bruise her softness.

"Mnmm mhmm, oh, oh, mhmm."

Hovey wedged a knee onto the table when its legs stuttered against the floor. Now he could feel vibrations in the wood. Determined, she increased the pressure on her sex. The sensitive yoni willed it so, begged for more. She rocked into the hard edge and lifted slightly to rake up the entire soft cove. The bud inflamed most – it smashed against the table recklessly, wild to explode.

No detour. No lull. Only speeding with abandon – Jane's young erotic heart, hasty and eager as ever.

The crest approached, where disbelief vanishes, whelmed by certainty. With one gigantic intake of breath, eyes wide with sharp surprise to achieve, she arched over.

"Ohhno oh uh oh uh oh oh." And ... "Oh!"

Her body quivered against the wooden edge. A scarlet flush appeared across her chest. She screamed again.

"Unh-ooohhhh."

A stream of liquids slushed onto the table. Her hands grasped breasts, squeezing as if to sink the rush into them. Her torso jerked violently. Yet not once did they break the bond of sight through which sensuality flowed, while shuddering ran its course.

"Fuck," she whispered, head shaking back and forth in awe. "Fuck. Fuck." Hips swayed against the table to set satisfaction deep.

Her breath grew rich, her aspect full of genuine shyness, amused confession, and outright pride of carnal greed – all at once.

"Your face is beautiful, Jane."

An arrow. She flooded with dark passion from his words. Her hands ceased grasping breasts. Her arms reached around to surround her body. She held herself comforted.

"I believe you."

The tableau held for seconds – until a fundamental sigh signaled an end.

Then, "Hither."

Hovey circled the table. Jane fled – shy, hesitating – to a corner where an angle separated kitchen from bedroom. She folded her arms into herself and spun front-wise into the niche. Hovey arrived behind, framing her with hands against the wall, not touching.

"What a brazen one she is," Jane whispered.

"No shame in it."

"No."

She turned fast and threw her arms around his neck, pulling him in hard. Jane exclaimed from the shock of her flesh on his, "Oh." They squirmed in the splendor of it. Kissing. Whispering nonsense. Furtive glances that confessed 'sex.'

"Yes," she said, approving of the world. "Yes," nodding with flared nostrils and wet eyes.

She pushed him away, clutched his trousers at the waist and yanked them down to the floor. With a whooping yell she smashed them back together. The phallus nestled into her belly.

Jane threw back her head, bellowing, "Oh for the love of sex!"

He made her spin back around to the wall. His arms circled to cross her body, pulling them tight back to front. His mouth settled at her left ear.

"You love it more than any woman. And you are so fast, Jane."

"I swear, Hovey, I felt bold *and* shy!" Amazed amusement, words barely clinging to the tongue. "Is that possible with such a brazen one?"

"Shy is not shame."

"Appears," she said. One of his favorite words. "I like you watching me. I like teasing you. Maybe I'll go too far, a second later I'm thrown on the floor, a hand on my neck, legs pushed open ... penetrated."

"How you talk."

"I want it."

"Taken hard on the floor?"

"Yes. I am not afraid."

"Your table trick was grand to watch, Jane."

"You never looked down."

"No."

"How?"

"I promised myself another go, soon. Ten minutes watching your fingers and the wetness."

Jane shuddered. "In?"

"Yes, shiny, wet, slipping in."

"Oh."

"Your fingers swimming."

She shook imagining it. Opening thighs just so. Lips all puffy. Agony to expose. He will see in. Everything sliding and slishing in warm liquids. My fingers slipping into the orifice. With him watching.

She wiggled her bottom.

"Please, Hovey."

"Turn to me. Unfold. Show your body." He backed away.

She rotated to face him. Her hands crossed at the base of her neck, then slid down, revealing smooth shoulders. They paused in place, a display of modesty. Then they uncrossed and swirled around her breasts. She contained them, letting the tips peek out through spread fingers. Then down her abdomen, sweeping in a dancer's gesture.

Soon her hands hung at hip level, to the side, away. Jane's carriage came erect, offered forward, simply and ordinarily naked.

"I will learn to do that better," she said, head lowered. She swayed.

"You do it well."

She looked up. "It tingles to show my body."

Hovey froze. The prospect of it stopped all else for the thrill in his imagination – his women had been ashamed or jaded. She caught on, let gravitas fill her intent.

"Exposing. Letting you see. Naked. Oh, there's a naked girl just there …"

He turned away. Jane whispered, "…his cock will get hard when she shows herself, yes? Every time she uncovers, yes? When her breasts become bare? Yes. She tingles in this, to make the beast come alive."

She raised her voice to a perfect tone.

"That woman is me," she said. "I am the naked girl in your world, Hovey. In your bed."

Jane grew urgent, speaking praise for the forcefulness of a man's fire, for the fright the stiff phallus wrought. Using her poet's words and passion, she told her hunger for hard and furious cock. Hovey took all in, standing rock steady on the earth.

"It chases me, throws me down, penetrates me," she said.

Now he looked in her eyes. "Yes."

"I'm so greedy for it, Hovey, you can't know. For cock. Rage of cock on me."

He ordered her to turn away yet again and place her hands on the wall. His mouth resumed its danger, an inch from hers.

"Your students should never guess this."

She smiled, with a blushing cheek aside his face.

"Are you sure I must always be naked, sir?"

"Yes."

"But I want to wear a Sunday dress buttoned all the way up. With a shift under. Petticoats. A silk corset. Knickers and beautiful stockings."

"I want you naked."

"Why, sir? Would you have me humiliated all the time?"

"So you cannot run away."

"That's not the reason."

The real reason insinuated itself against her low back and bottom. She pushed back against it. She could sense hunger in his face, even with her back to him, even at an angle. Familiar now, to make a man blind with arousal, merely from being naked in his presence.

A moment suspended, the warmth rising from bodies carried subtle aroma.

"You have an after-scent, Jane."

"What?"

"Your skin. Taste and scent. Different after finishing."

"Oh."

His mouth fit to the curve of her shoulder. Jane jerked away with a bellow. But she slid back, breathing hard. He kissed next to the first one.

"There," he whispered.

"Oh."

"And here."

Jane endured torment for minutes. Faced into the corner, hands flat on the wall above her head, she permitted him to caress wherever, contain however, trail maddeningly more ethereal fingertip touches forever. His hands moved delicately. Kisses across her back, and down. She squirmed with incitement of electrified nerve ends, to avoid the feather brushings on skin – yet beseeched for them never to cease. Every kiss melted salts and oils deposited during her self-pleasure at the corner-edge of the table.

He would not miss any by taste or scent.

Jane groaned and shuddered.

The trail returned up and he whispered between one feather-kiss and another.

"Oh, this girl perfume."

He slipped one hand under the mane of black hair and eased it to the side, then over the shoulder to fall down in front. His exquisite kisses fell on the nape of her neck. Jane hissed with pleasure.

He whispered, "I will never let you put clothes on again."

"I can't go to church naked."

"You must abstain from church."

His mouth attended her shoulder. His sightline included peering over to her front.

"The table? It has been anointed."

Jane giggled. "Yes, splashed good."

"Drink water in abundance Jane, for anointing. And to remain slippery."

She groaned. "Oh yes, wet and soft and slippery inside."

"That sound when fingers touch the wet ..." He paused. "Make it now."

Jane's right hand removed from the wall and descended, fitting the vee. The music of stirred waters arose. She sighed.

"Oh. Oh."

She brought her hand up for them to see. It glistened in the last light coming in from the windows. The distinct scent of femme arousal grew.

"I like being ready for you," she said.

She moved fingers to let strands of wet span between. The play of her anointed fingers fascinated. She renewed the wet, and offered the sight of glistening threads between.

"Move you hand down and behind," he said.

He guided her hand in position to cup and contain one half her bottom.

"Hold it gently."

His left arm wrapped around her waist, ready to take up weight.

"Lift your leg up the wall."

He helped by sliding his right hand under the rising thigh.

"Pull open, Jane."

"Thus, I will be entered?"

"Yes."

"From behind, he ravishes her, not to see."

"You like it this way."

"Yes, so I can have my extreme feelings, Hovey. They are too immoderate for your eyes."

"Pull open a little more."

"Privacy to not let you see my turmoil and hopes."

"I will seek them."

"Seek them."

"... the lips. Are they closed?"

"They are wet."

"Are they closed?"

She nodded.

"Get one finger close, gather, pull gently."

"Oh ...."

"Exposed. Open."

"Yes."

"When show your body naked, I know this may be offered to me."

"I will always offer it."

The cock slipped in. Little whispers from both with tender flesh parting to accept hard organ. The confident strokes began. Immediately Jane began to groan, so aroused by their play and teasing she could not be silent on thrusts.

Hovey held his woman in his arms from behind, entering her body to the burn of their ardor, his mouth near her ear.

"Tell an extreme wish," he said.

"The hard thing?"

"Yes?"

"It penetrates all my insides."

"Yes."

"Aim for my heart."

7:03

They sat on their chairs on the porch before sundown. Jane had pulled the flower-print dress over her body again. Her feet were bare.

"I must make you look at two things now, Jane."

"What?"

"You see how strong your spell is on me."

She smiled. "Yes."

"It is more than you know. I am fierce to possess you, Jane. To have you, yes. But to possess you."

She looked proud, and could have answered.

He continued, "This I say knowing you cannot be

possessed to the bottom of your soul. Ever."

"I cannot."

"It is a man's challenge to try, nevertheless."

Jane sat in the radiance of it, knowing he would say more.

He said, flatly, "Also, fending off you trying to possess me."

Now she laughed aloud and nodded.

"This greed for possessing will make us fight."

"Yes. I am not afraid to fight over you."

Hovey pointed to the west, where the taller of the two hills hid the descending sun. It was about three hundred feet high.

"My ambition on you is big as that hill."

Before she could react, he stood them up, took her hand and led her to the east end of the porch, and pointed to the massive mountain visible around the corner of the building to the north.

"That is Bear Mountain. Over ten thousand feet. As big as my life ambition, Jane. To make something important, useful in this world, in this life. To be rich in it. Wealthy. And satisfied as a man."

"Yes, Hovey."

"Some men push other men aside to win, and not fairly. Not honest. They push their women aside, ignore them or humiliate them –"

"Or beat them."

There was a profound moment when both let the rage of this rise ... and recede.

"I will not do that to you."

"I know."

"Jane, can you know what I am saying? Which mountain is bigger?"

She nodded slowly.

"Do not distract me. Do not break in on my solitude when I need it. Do not shame me for being like stone sometimes."

"Like granite."

"Yes. Yet ... know this. I seek both. It is not one or the other Jane Cady Whitfield. It is both."

"You are safe. I will be busy with my ambitions. All my ambitions."

A silence.

"What is the other damn thing you are forcing me to look at?"

"That day in the East, your family ..."

"Yes?"

"You faced death."

"Yes."

"... must ask you about it one more time."

"Why? I've got sex! You seem to like sex. We have sex. We are chasing the shade down the street with sex."

"I need to know if you survived without praying to God. Or raging at God."

"Don't, Hovey, don't. Don't make me think of it. Don't make me. Take me in your arms. Comfort me. Please."

"No."

"Please hold me."

"No. Tell it."

"You are cruel. Why are you making me?"

"Tell."

Jane rallied. Sorrowful poetry welled in her breast.

"Sitting there, rocking, weeping. The pain stabbing me one second, then sick with nausea. The agony of seeing it was real, that such a thing could happen. Then,

all of a sudden, I went empty. I remember that. Empty.
Silence all around. I stood up and went to their bedsides.
First my father. I didn't recognize him, but then the full
remembrance of his kindness flooded in. Like a stone
falling on me, I understood he had filled our home with
prosperity and protection. I loved my father. Something
seeped in the door of our home, something foul,
destroyed him, heartless. I went into the next room and
stared with horror at my brother's body. I screamed
against the walls of his room. Then, a tender memory,
several of them. He once told me I was 'a girl like a boy
like a girl.' I'll never forget that. When I turned away from
his bed, I thought a giant anvil hit the ground. Then,
Virginia. My mother. A stab of sorrow put me on the
floor. A fucking knife in my heart. The worst thing of my
life. How could she be dead, with her womb that bore
me, her breasts filled with milk. Warm. I could feel her
embrace and all the love in it, filled up and giving. And
every wise thing she said, every hard thing she made me
do for strength. She cannot be dead. Then I stood up.
They were still dead."

"No hope to change the world's law."

"I had to look, Hovey. To honor them. Honor truth."

"You did not pretend about heaven?"

"No."

"Ever?"

"My loved ones lay flat dead in that house, Hovey.
Oblivion. For eternity."

"Jane ..."

"Oblivion. May I be struck by an avalanche if I ever
pretend otherwise. That is the world's law." Hovey stared
at her. "I did not pray to God or rage at God."

"I believe you."

"Compared to reality, God is small."

Hovey froze. She did not rush on, letting the magnitude of such an utterance bounce off the walls of the ranch house. Jane watched his face carefully.

"You mean that?"

"Yes, Hovey."

"Blasphemy."

"Yes, I know. There are things worse than blasphemy ... if God turns out to be real, I'll ask him why he is so small and mean, killing innocents like that. I've asked people about it. Their answers are even smaller and meaner."

"People do not face oblivion as you do, Jane. I had to ask, to be sure."

"I will never let that moment diminish, Hovey, staring at oblivion," she said. "To pretend their souls are alive somewhere, so the pain is less."

"Do not diminish. The world will hate you for your pride. Live fierce, for defiance."

"Yes."

Then Jane turned on him, stood utterly still, staring him down, intention like a roaring wave.

"I found my friend on the floor, shot through the forehead. Pretend was nowhere to be found in that moment. As you say, 'flat dead'."

"Oh ..."

"Ramon saved my life two times. He also introduced me to Marguerite. Now he was no more. The pain was worse than that knife in my side. Yet I did not pretend."

Hovey opened his hurting soul for a few seconds. Jane saw. When his stern countenance returned, she knew that no more true and adamant certainty might be found of the finality of death in its majesty.

She forgave him for forcing this conversation. "These two things you needed to know before you promise yourself to me."

"Yes, Jane."

Then, Hovey made jest without smiling.

"I have not looked to the sky and asked Ramon for advice about you."

Jane did not laugh.

"We did not choose to be born," Hovey said.

"No."

"We cannot forestall death."

"No."

"This world is all there is."

"Yes."

"No 'other place'."

"No."

"No exit. No outside. Cannot get out because there is nothing else. Anywhere."

"No."

"Jane, this is eternity."

Shocked silent. She spun in place on the porch. Eyes huge, she stared into his, then turned her head away and stared into space.

"We are in eternity?"

"Yes."

"Naked for eternity?"

"Yes."

She turned to him.

"Tease and touch and kiss and coo?"

"And finish sex, Jane."

"Oh ..."

"Scream against the walls for it."

"I will scream ten times to your one, poor man."

His wise visage said there must be justice somewhere, to not let her get away with such a score.

"Finish sex and begin sex and finish sex," she said. "And laugh in bed together. Each become richer than the other, for fun? Watch out, I will make something big, Hovey. Build something. Do something big and difficult. Money."

"That we do for revenge."

Their gaze held strong and grew wide. Jane moved to him, put her body against him, arms around his neck. The emotions of embrace rose magnificently.

"To live for defiance."

They kissed it true. Jane could not weep for the rapture of it. Then her joy turned to jolly.

"So you'll be smelling like cattle for the foreseeable future?"

"Yes. For all eternity."

7:41

Jane made an entry in her journal ...

"He has taken the same shelter as I – the beat of two hearts within – absent a void without."

8:03

Nearing sunset, Hovey conducted a closer inspection of the stove and chimney system, suspecting some small thing to be affecting its working.

Of a sudden, he realized Jane's outside walk had been quite long. He moved out onto the porch. There, he found her casually enjoying the air at dusk, but also with expectation. She wore the flower-print dress and riding boots. Both horses stood by, tethered to the railing, with no saddles. She smiled knowingly, took Grey's lead in

hand, and leapt onto his back. With one last glance at
Hovey, she trotted the steed out across the yard.

He followed. They crossed out of the fences,
westward, and traversed the flat, soon reaching the base of
the large hill. Not a word passed between them. Jane led
the way up, familiar from having previously ascended. At
the top, three hundred feet above the homestead, they
dismounted, tethering their horses to a fallen tree. Jane let
Hovey make a full circle taking in the view. He stopped
and brought his attention to her steady visage.

With the sun on the rim of the west, Jane painted a
picture of the land all around built up into a fine
prosperous ranch and farm. They had a small lake just
there, a grove of fruit trees near it, and his cattle roaming
everywhere – although fenced off from the homestead. A
magnificent house with veranda on three sides, windows
filled with light, the sound of music floating in the air
from a studio standing alone, with one wall that could
open to form a performance stage. Jane told of a dream of
floating slowly in the morning light, in balloons filled
with heated air, such as delighted people in Europe.

"We will sail over the land," she whispered. "So
beautiful."

"Jane ..."

"We could make it together, own it together, but not
be married."

"What?"

"Not married. We each have big things to do. We are
not having children. We should never melt out lives
together to do ordinary things. It ruins sex and affection
between people to do that."

"Some people."

"Many. A hideous silence down the streets of the

land, when there should be noise from every bedroom."

"They are busy with children."

"They can wait until the children are fast asleep."

"Jane ..."

"We should live close to the fire, Hovey. To be burned by the urge for life."

"I see."

"I don't want a house husband, and I will never be a wife."

"I believe it."

"You agreed we don't have ordinary sex."

"We do not."

"On fire," she said, a whisper with awe in it.

"For how long?"

"We should each have our own acres. Own fences. Own house. Then I could surprise sneak into yours at night and slip under the covers, naked."

"All this because you finish so hard? So fast?"

"Yes. Heaven in a bed. I want sex with you in paradise."

"It could fade, Jane."

"No."

"Yes. Sex could fade."

"Your two women died before you could make love forever."

Hovey shuddered, with eyes wide open. "What?"

"Did it fade?"

"Yes, with one of them."

"After you promised yourself to her, did she stay eager and skilled to please you?"

Hovey stood silent. Jane let the point sink deep.

"Don't believe sex has to die," she said after a moment. "You don't know."

"People say it."

"If you only have me – no other woman – sometimes only every few weeks, and we live with the solitude of the self in between ..."

"Sex would be wild and wicked."

"Gentle sometimes and fierce sometimes."

"Yes."

"Sometimes take me hard, up against a wall. Sometimes gentle. I want both ways, Hovey."

"Yes."

"I will do something every day, something tempting. Something sweet, yet full of sex at the same time. To show you my loveliness, my girl happiness, as no one else in this world will ever see – but with hunger in it. Shy ... and shameless."

"Oh ..."

"I will whisper the mischievous things that wake the mighty thing. I know how, Hovey. I know your rousing. I will drive you mad to have me."

He nodded.

Jane paused. She took a step closer. The moon shone a erotic glint in her eyes.

"I've made you hard right now."

"Yes."

Jane smiled like the best girl of Miss Honeyhurst's.

"I will stay slender."

"Oh."

"I know you want that."

"Yes."

"Take me in your arms, wrap them around my body. I will bend into you, give my breasts, my belly, my mouth to be kissed. Everything soft, like a girl, for you to put your hard body on. You will feel me melting for it, pleading to be entered. Every day, at least once, I will give myself to you ... with intention anew."

"This is how you want to spend eternity?"

"Yes."

"Sex?"

"To build something worthy through the actions of my will. A magnificent ranch. A school of my own. And to watch your kingdom grow. And sex!"

"To keep us strong."

"We must be interesting people, and mischievous."

"And away from each other sometimes."

"Even the Bible tells us to abstain for a week every month."

"It does?"

"Yes."

"This fire needs one more thing," he said.

"Hovey, I feel the pain of living and dying. If our eternities fit together side by side, one of us will look upon the dead body of the other."

That stopped them. Did not scare them. He broke the silence.

"We should die together from orgasm."

"That would be best!"

"You are hiding from one thing needed, Jane."

"What?"

"Nineteen years old. Caught a man in her web. Giddy with finishing. No slowing down."

"Yes. So what?"

"Blind and deaf, it appears."

"So?"

Hovey showed the irony in his eyes, turning to fetch the leather lead of his horse. He leapt on. As he eased past with his eyes holding hers, his sober and challenging visage mystified. He said nothing, leaving her standing fast. Urging his mount, he headed downhill.

As he trotted forward from the base of the hill, a wailing scream of shock and exultation rained down from above. Soon, Jane rode madly past, Grey straining to match her urgency. She did not look over at him.

Arriving at the ranch house, Hovey found Jane standing in the middle of the room waiting, impish and alight. She drew tall. The hem of the flower-print dress crept an inch up her bare legs. The s-curve of her torso formed.

His aggressive impetus exploded. At his first step, her hand rose in a gesture of staying. She did not say their "stop" – yet he did. He tried again. As soon as he moved, Jane's hand rose another two inches and her visage tightened. He stopped.

There in the gleam of her eye, there in the tilt of her head, Jane asked the fated question.

Hovey met her gaze with no less monumental weight than in all their times together, a stoic mountain refusing to dissolve under a million years of rain. It was the visage adored by her liquid softness.

The tension held for a second. Several seconds.

Then, a shudder down his spine. A slight squeeze of the eyes. And at long last, a tiny bob of the head.

"Was not seeking. Found."

Jane roared with jubilation. She ran into his arms screaming his name. They told the truth, each once. They embraced as true lovers for the first time and kissed it deep.

9:41 p.m.
Now a conversation was desperately needed about

how much is too much. Saying it.

"Never say it again."

"Hovey, I'm going to say it a million times."

"Never."

They were sitting on the bed with a cut-up apple on a plate between them. The situation was critical, but there was mirth in their smiles.

"Don't you think I'll get irritated? A female starving for proclamations stalking you? I can pout like a girl, Hovey."

"A small price to pay."

"I'm going to say it now."

"I forbid it."

Jane sat up straight. She turned ominous.

"Ok, then. Watch out now. And listen. I'm going to say it one more time, but due to your cowardly self, I'll not say it again, ever."

"Good," he said.

"You won't hear it from me, after this, Hovey. Seriously. This is it. Last time. Here goes ..."

He held up one finger for her to wait. He sighed. Jane saw signs of the businessman preparing a counteroffer. It happened so fast, however, she was not prepared. He spoke.

"I love you."

Jane fell backwards onto the blankets, gurgling with shock. She bounced back up, greeted by the absolute stony countenance of her man.

"Say it fifty more times," was all she could think of.

"No."

"Life is not going to be boring for us."

"Jane, when we say it, no insistence."

"Insistence?"

"No demands on it for the other to say it back right then."

"Oh."

Jane considered this unusual idea. She was a prime suspect for breaking that rule, but with a light heart advised herself to accept.

"Is that how you said it just now?"

"Yes. It wells up and spills out. We do not look for the other to say it. Or ask them to."

"Well hell, William Bennis Hovey. What the hell?"

Hovey waited. If anything, he became more stone-faced than ever. Like Buddha under a tree.

Jane tried on the attitude. No obligation. Just a woman feeling her emotions, and the wonderful urge to say one aloud. Nothing attached.

"I love you," she said.

9:53 p.m.

An hour of conversation kept the mood aglow. They did not need to visit the pains left behind. Jane showed Hovey, who was literate, how she was taught to read as a child, and that she hoped college would confirm this method. She persuaded him to run out the details of his plan for the coming year to keep the herd healthy and valuable. Many times, Jane overflowed – she leaned in with offered lips to be kissed.

11:15

Abruptly, Hovey slipped on his riding clothes. Standing near in her flower dress, Jane thought it odd. Little did she know he deemed it important to ride out to gauge conditions surrounding the homestead at this hour. This was a natural and wise thing for a range-savvy man.

"Why are you dressing for the herds, sir?"

"Ready to defend the ranch."

"Really?"

"From a horde of Yankees raiding to get their college girl out of captivity."

Jane snorted. "I'll just walk out all nude, strutting and prideful, they won't want me after that."

"Guess the real reason."

"You are going outside?"

"Yes."

"The kingliness of being fully dressed, riding fences of his kingdom, returning to the castle to find an eager naked girl running around, ready for him."

"Yes."

"He could barge in from winter range ..."

"And such a girl will dance around, brushing off the snow, and the cold will make her skin glow."

In one smooth motion, Jane pulled the dress up and off her body, letting it crumple to the floor around her beautiful feet. "Okay, you are dressed for battle, and I am stark naked. You've got your silly setup, Hovey."

He walked out.

11:25

Jane retrieved the dress, pulled it over her torso, and sat at the table to write.

"There is a solitude which each and every one of us carries with us, more imperious than the ice-cold mountains, more profound than the midnight sea; the solitude of self. The self our choices and courage have created. In that solemn solitude, which knows the finite borders of reality, yet considers them infinite in despite, each soul lives alone in an eternity." *

[*Jane channeled her remembrance of the most important paragraph in the most important writing of i-feminist Elizabeth Cady Stanton in her essay of 1892, "The Solitude of the Self." With her mother, Jane attended Stanton's reading of it before the US Senate Judiciary Committee in Washington when Jane was sixteen. She modified some phrases to best reflect her convictions.]

Jane and Hovey entwined twice more before dawn.

Waking, whispering, and kissing, Jane compelled
Hovey to perform and accept gentle eroticisms she yet
believed no cowboy would endure in bed with a woman.
She roamed his body with torturous kisses, as he had done
to hers earlier. Each in turn took the organ of the other in
immersing oral union, until juices flowed.

After a sharp verbal duel over 'possessing,' he became
a hunter running her down in the dead of night when she
attempted to feign serenity and unavailability out on the
porch, scampering away on the balls of bare feet. This
ended with her bent into the wooden deck, immobile,
helpless under the driving strength put on her by a
warrior claiming victory. Hands twined in her hair
controlled utterly. When she grunted in rebellion, he
yanked her into a new position, body pinned in place, and
penetrated her open sex, thrusting relentlessly until
mourning doves woke in the trees and took flight in
terror of her screams.

~~~~~

They lay exhausted in bed. Dawn readied nearby. Jane's voice rang out with happy exasperation.

"Sex!"

"Yes."

"Oh sex!"

"Yes."

"But I will never marry."

"Nor I."

Jane bubbled. "We could be lying."

"No."

"Might." She spurted and giggled again. "Do you like my idea of two houses."

"Yes."

"So I can sneak into yours every night?"

"Yes, Jane."

"We are so tricky. We have to be."

"Pretend to be virgin one night."

She gulped a big breath.

"Oh. Oh. I felt that right below my belly button. To give myself as a virgin to you again. Yes."

Hovey sat up. The embrace fell apart.

"I have to hush the dream now, Jane."

That had to happen. She was brave.

"Go ahead."

Hovey looked at her with squinting eyes.

"It is just some cows, some grass, some water. But I will be sharp with battle for a year."

"Go ahead."

She sat up, filled with drama. The bed sheet slipped off one breast. Her right arm swept up and behind to draw the cascade of black hair around her neck to fall down her back. Jane's intention elevated from the man nearby, separate ambition and purpose glinting in her eyes.

"I will teach the children to read."

August 12, 1895
Monday
6:00 a.m.
Riding into Silver City

One mile north of the ranch, Jane and Hovey came to a stop at the "Jane" sign. She slid off Grey, tore the board off the stake, which she yanked from the ground and tossed behind a bush. Let there be no hint of anything interesting down the south path for anyone's inquisitiveness.

Jane tucked the sign into her saddle bag, with some affection for the irony it possessed. From the saddle, Hovey spoke when she looked up.

"There is a place halfway between here and my range on the Gila. Halfway. A miner made a camp-house at the top of the pass, a few hundred feet off, you would ride right by if you did not know it was there. The cabin is near a spring, the source of the Lithy River. Hardly ever anyone there. About a six-hour ride for each of us."

"William!"

Hovey nearly fell off his horse.

"Oh, William! Did you look in it on your way here?"

"Yes."

"You had to deliberately leave the path, climb up?"

"Yes. You cannot see the cabin from the trail."

He was shaking. She savored the effect for seconds, before granting mercy.

"Don't worry, Hovey, I'll never call you that again."

"Wicked vixen of a woman."

"Only six hours in the saddle?"

"Yes."

Jane's eyes grew wise. "I shall make a calendar of my fertility."

She did not voice her feeling, although it welled up, for the fine silent strategies her man would make, surely, all the way into the oncoming twentieth century. She pretended that was their destination, once she regained the saddle and urged Grey forward.

epilogue
April 1897

gold

April 11, 1897
Sunday
8:20 a.m.
Jane's Ranch
Seven miles west of Silver City, NM

With a sigh befitting so significant a remembrance, Jane returned to 1897 reality. The sun flooded the bedroom. Her attention turned to the box on her lap. She opened it carefully.

First, the white cotton flower-print dress, worn only once since their grand collision nearly two years ago, on the first anniversary of the first day of her womanhood – it was ceremonial now. It was astonishing, given the extremes of that day and night, that the dress was in one piece. At the bottom of the box, the famous sign pointing the direction "a jane" might be located in the wild. Last, the journal of their first year together, filled with love and sex. With bittersweet tenderness she opened it to the first entry.

"No!"

Jane slammed the book shut. She jumped up from the bed.

The rest of the morning found her discharging ammunition in fierce practice with the rifle bought last year – soon after new window glazing. She reloaded fast. Also, roping, first from ground level, then at a pace with Grey swirling around the yard in obedience to her commands. At length, she leapt from the horse and took the stance of a cowboy foreman forbidding miscreant behavior in the crew.

"He lost his foreman. Whatever Peterson could do, I

can do." Jane Cady Whitfield stood unyielding in the sun until certain of it.

April 12, 1897
Monday
7:00 a.m.

Jacob and Heather rode up on their buckboard. As they jumped down, Jane started strong.

"Jacob, can you hold tight for a shock?"

"Yes, ma'am."

"I need to go from here, for two weeks. I need someone to stay and care for this ranch. I'm offering you and Heather this homestead, with pay, for two weeks."

"Jane!" cried Heather.

"Oh."

Jane let Jacob dwell a moment. Heather stared at her husband.

"To stay here every night for two weeks? Just do the chores and milkin'?"

"Yes, Jacob. And your fix list, yes. That big fence job, get that done. But sleep in your bed out yonder, not in my bed. Okay?"

Heather flushed. Her eyes lit up and glistened.

"Well, Heather's folks expect us. And I have things to do. Work for my uncle and a few such and such chores. Maybe I can't."

Jane pulled two coins from her pocket and set them on the table. Gold.

"These come from my savings, and I want them to go to you now. Put this first twenty in your pocket at the end of the first week, and this other twenty to stay right on this table until the day I come back and we settle up."

The young couple stared at the fortune shining bright on the rough tabletop. When they finally looked up, they met Jane's serious visage pouring out her will.

"And here's the five you expected by tomorrow," she said, handing Jacob a small silver coin. "Tell your uncle 'no' for two weeks, Jacob."

Heather's eyes melted into Jane. Jacob looked off to the side, fighting the yes and no.

"I could ride into town and back a few days?"

"Yes. You won't leave Heather alone here after dark."

"It's planting time," said Heather.

"Can you plant the garden, Heather?"

"Yes, I do believe I can. You'll tell me things."

"Yes. This morning. In an hour I'll be gone."

"Where are you going?"

Jane's spurs sang out as she took a step forward.

"To sleep in the trail bed of the one I love."

After

As the new century approached, Jane and Hovey strove in their separate life-projects with determination to prosper ... and to love uniquely, fiercely, shunning the restraints and disapprovals of the world.

In the fall of 1903, they engaged in a contest of wills, with neither slipping naked into the bed of the other for a week.

The following year their son, Adam, was born. A princess, Laurel, followed two years later. On the birth certificates, evidence that Hovey had won the big battle – the children bore his name, and in the lockbox for important papers a marriage certificate could be found resting quietly.

Just as Jane forgot the pain of childbirth upon holding a newborn in her arms, her pain from Hovey having his way about "marriage" diminished to nothing – because her fear that domestic life would destroy their furious lovemaking melted away. For decades after, this was so, because when the beautiful children fell asleep, noise erupted in the bedroom.

Jane lived until the middle of the Twentieth Century, coming to know her granddaughter, Caroline, who married Aleksy Wojciechowski in 1964. From that union came Georg Wojciechowski, whose dramatic marriage to Lin Xin Qian of China produced a remarkable daughter, Xia, in 2004.

When Xia reached fertility and began looking at boys with intensity, Lin passed on the lovely box to her ... the one holding her great-great-grandmother's white flower-painted dress, a journal of a year of triumphant love in bed, and a sign pointing to where "a jane" might be found in the wilderness.

For more on the progeny of
William Bennis Hovey and Jane Cady Whitfield,
visit the home page of John Caedan
to read *The Preludes* and *The White Sky*

JohnCaedan.com | ThePreludes.com | TheWhiteSky.com

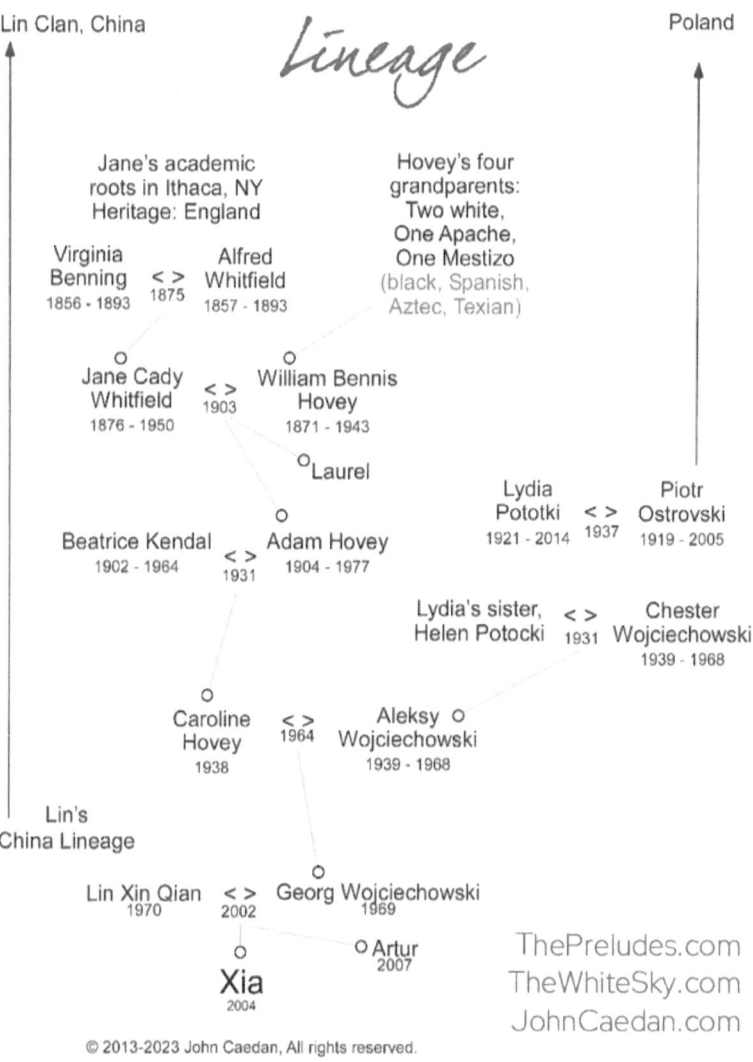

Lin Clan, China

Lineage

Poland

Jane's academic
roots in Ithaca, NY
Heritage: England

Hovey's four
grandparents:
Two white,
One Apache,
One Mestizo
(black, Spanish,
Aztec, Texian)

Virginia
Benning
1856 - 1893

< >
1875

Alfred
Whitfield
1857 - 1893

Jane Cady
Whitfield
1876 - 1950

< >
1903

William Bennis
Hovey
1871 - 1943

Laurel

Lydia
Pototki
1921 - 2014

< >
1937

Piotr
Ostrovski
1919 - 2005

Beatrice Kendal
1902 - 1964

< >
1931

Adam Hovey
1904 - 1977

Lydia's sister,
Helen Potocki

< >
1931

Chester
Wojciechowski
1939 - 1968

Caroline
Hovey
1938

< >
1964

Aleksy
Wojciechowski
1939 - 1968

Lin's
China Lineage

Lin Xin Qian
1970

< >
2002

Georg Wojciechowski
1969

Artur
2007

Xia
2004

ThePreludes.com
TheWhiteSky.com
JohnCaedan.com

books by
j.j.kirnan

Touch Me Again
Jane Nineteen
Andrés + Mila
Love in Bed

jjkirnan.com

About this Edition

Illustrations composed and rendered
by j.j.kirnan

Cover font "Allison"
by Robert Leuschke
for Google Fonts

Text font "EB Garamond"
Designed by Georg Duffner, Octavio Pardo
for Google Fonts

Text block style:
Ragged right justification, non-hyphenated.
While writers are strictly advised to format
their texts with equal length lines,
I inquired if that was true for poetry.
No.